RIVER STONE

Book One of **The Burning Days**

RIVER STONE

RACHEL HENNESSY

MidnightSun

First published 2019 by MidnightSun Publishing Pty Ltd
PO Box 3647, Rundle Mall, SA 5000, Australia.
www.midnightsunpublishing.com

Cover design by Kim Lock
Internal design by Zena Shapter

Typeset in Copperplate, Gill Sans and Bookman Old Style.

Printed and bound in Australia by Griffin Press. The papers used by MidnightSun in the manufacture of this book are natural, recyclable products made from wood grown in sustainable plantation forests.

A catalogue record for this book is available from the National Library of Australia

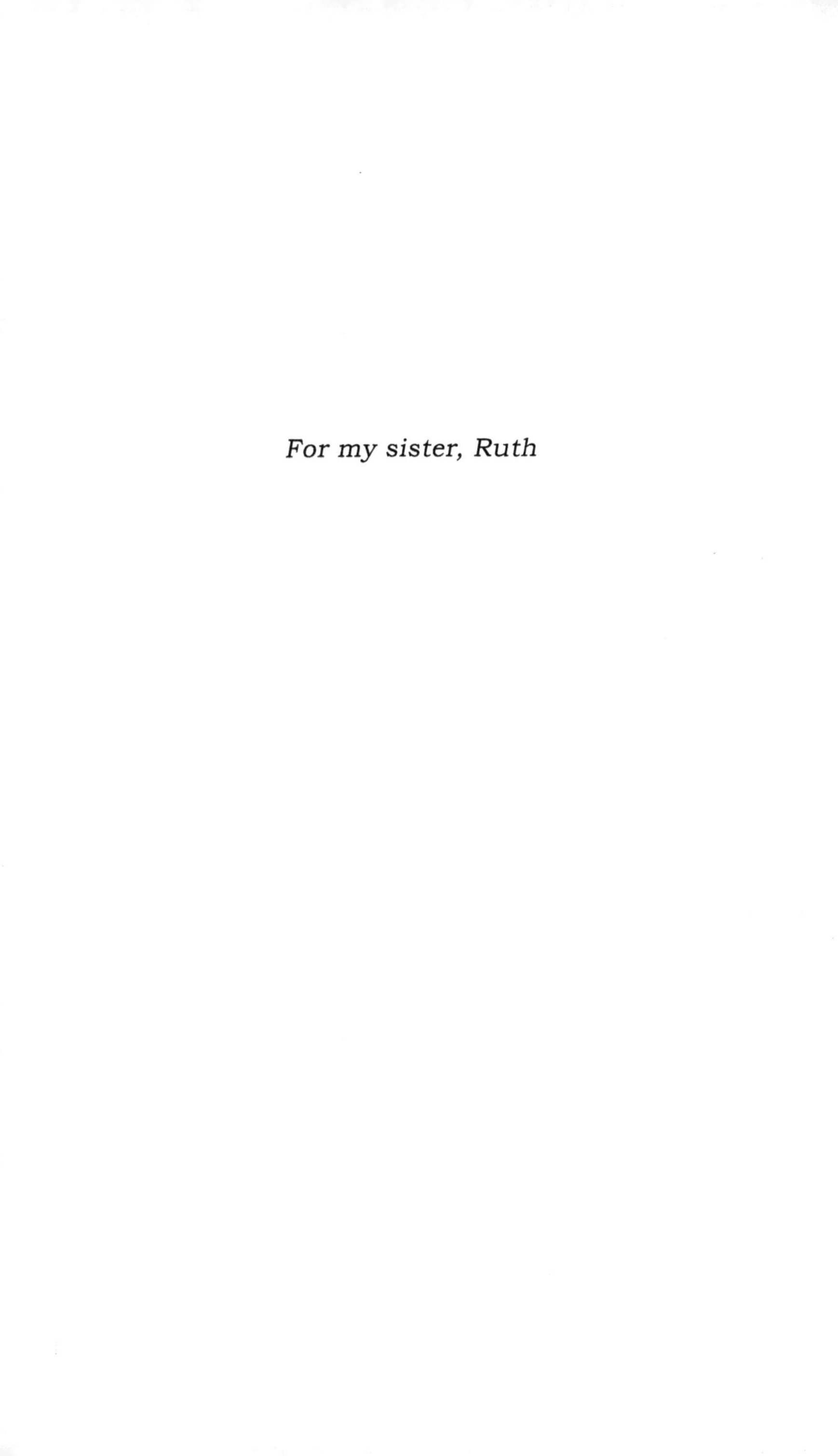

For my sister, Ruth

'But if there were so few humans left,
why did they not stay together?'
'Because they chose not to.'
'And why did they choose not to?'
'Because they were human.'

PART ONE

1

'Hold still,' Theodore whispers and I close my eyes.

I try not to tense, to anticipate the pain. My father has talked to me about staying relaxed throughout, to make it hurt less. I can feel Theodore behind me, the heat of the carved river stone in his gloved hand.

I bite my lip as the stone sears into my shoulder blade. *By the rivers*, it hurts … but I don't cry out. I squeeze my hands tightly together, forcing myself to stop the tears threatening to fall.

The circle and the three waves are being branded into my skin. I smell the scorched flesh but still I don't move, don't flinch away from the rock becoming one with me. In my mind I see the cool water, the beautiful clear stream I love. I imagine myself diving into that pool. I swim to the bottom, to the sandy bed where the river stones shimmer like silver.

'You are done.'

I open my eyes, flexing my clenched fingers and pushing down a wave of nausea. I turn to face Theodore. His long grey hair hangs down on either side of his face and he stares at me with his great, all-seeing orbs. He places his hands on my shoulders.

'Pandora.' I feel the significance of him using my whole name. I am a legend, I have been told, a reminder of a woman who, long ago, opened a jar holding all the wickedness of the world, bringing horror and destruction. We have had our own horror and destruction; we call it The Burning. My parents have never explained why they chose such a name for me. It doesn't exactly bode well.

'Pandora, of the River People.'

Theodore looks at me for a little longer. He nods and I slowly turn from him. Ahead of me, standing at the other side of the Great Hall, my mother and father wait. The pain of the branding was intense but I have not cried or cowered or embarrassed them. They should be looking proud. Perhaps it is the smoke and the intense throbbing of my head, because they look worried. Perhaps, despite the physical rite I have just been through, they know this next is the part of the Blossoming I have trembled over the most.

Along the path tree-stump seats are arranged,

holding all the adults of our village. Only two are missing: the teacher, Rama, who will be watering the fields with the young ones, and today's sentry, Davern, who will be roaming the boundaries, keeping an eye out for dangers.

I walk towards my parents. I'm naked except for my goateep-skin pants but I don't feel shy, everyone has seen me before. In summer we don't bother covering ourselves. My mother tells me I will start to feel more self-conscious as I grow but, for now, my breasts are still small, I am almost a boy.

My mother is in her ceremonial dress, faded to white. It matches her skin, a strong contrast to my father's blackness. She holds a piece of the healing plant. I can see how she is desperate to run to me and offer a salve to my burn. My father has his hand on her arm, gently gripping her, holding her back. Draped over his other arm is the long dress I will now wear.

When I am in front of them, my mother walks behind me and rubs the end of the broken plant into the lines of the brand. It stings, then cools. The pain is still there, only now it feels deeper, less raw.

She returns to stand next to my father. I lean down and pull off my pants, trying to ignore the smarting every time I move my right arm. My father hands me the dress. I pull it over my head, the loose goateep-skin has been tanned and thinned over the last year, and it only has one shoulder, leaving the brand untouched. I can't help running my hands over the black fur. It's the most beautiful thing I've ever worn.

'Pan ... Pandora,' my mother begins. She isn't used to using my full name, like she wants to forget its heritage.

'Pandora,' she begins again, this time more confidently. 'You have reached your Blossoming and are now fully of the River People. Your father and I have considered long and hard on your future. Your father and I ...'

She takes my left hand and my father takes my right. They both hold hands. We become a circle, the same circle I've just had inscribed on my back. I want this circle never to be broken, for the three of us to be a family, just like this, as it has always been, for the last seventeen notches engraved into the Growing Tree. But, in the next moment, this is all over.

'We have chosen Matthew for you.'

I lie on my reed mat with my face turned toward the fire in our hut. My parents walked me here, giving me instructions to be still and drink water, before they returned to the hall to watch the Blossoming of my best friend, Fatima, and Matthew, Emmaline and Titus. This is all of us. Five of us reaching our Blossoming. Next year, there will be Fatima's sister, Cassie, and Matthew's brother, Christophe. Slowly, our village grows.

I wonder briefly if Emmaline's and Titus's ceremonies will be any different from mine; if our leader, Theodore, will do something exceptional for his beloved daughter and nephew, before I return to the depressing thoughts lodged inside my head since Matthew was named my Chosen.

I did not, as I worried I might, cry out or protest. I accepted the kiss both my parents gave me, one on each cheek. The three of us walked out of the hall, though no longer holding hands, to the sound of polite clapping. My attachment to Matthew does not come as a surprise to the rest of the village, we have been seen together enough, so they think it is natural.

It's only me who thinks it is not.

'We are very excited about this new phase of your life, Pan,' my mother said, as we walked.

'We are really proud of the way you handled the

Blossoming,' my father chimed in. 'You've accepted what is best.'

They were like a double-act of cheerfulness and I tried to smile, to fool them into thinking I was happy too.

It's my own fault. I have never been able to tell anyone how I feel about Matthew. Or, more accurately, how I *don't* feel about Matthew. What can I say that won't sound self-centred and petty? What does love have to do with the need to re-populate the land? What have my feelings got to do with saving us from extinction? When I was fourteen notches, my father told me he would never 'pair me off' with someone I didn't love but as my Blossoming approached he seemed to forget he had ever said such a thing.

'It's for the best,' he repeated, like a mantra. Maybe he is right.

I look up at the hairline crack in the mud-brick of our hut, running from halfway up the wall to the chimney, the same crack I have been waking up to for as long as I can remember. Outside, everything is strangely quiet. At this point in the day, I would normally be heavily into work: in the wheat fields; at the mill stone, helping to grind; at the pens, milking the goateeps; or out gathering, finding roots and berries. Always with Matthew and Fatima, helping to keep the boredom away, always a mix of tasks to ensure we would keep up the enthusiasm.

Our lessons with Rama give us another kind of work: learning how to read (I'm not so good at this) and about life long before The Burning. Learning about a time when people hardly spoke to one another, just used words on something called a 'screen' to tell each other what they thought; a time when there were machines to carry you from one side of the Earth to another; a time when food could be bought with 'money' from a wondrous place called a 'supermarket'. There's always been contention about these lessons. My mother, for one, has protested them, arguing against dwelling on the past, on failing to live in the present. So far, she continues to be overruled.

'If we don't know our history,' Rama says, 'we are doomed to repeat it.'

But I am glad not to have to listen to these lessons today or to have to work. I am grateful not to have to see Matthew yet, to understand how happy he is I've been named his Chosen and to have to hide how unhappy I am.

'Pan?'

Fatima is at the opening of our hut. Fatima?

Breaking the rules and coming to see me on Blossoming day? Things *are* changing.

'What are you doing here, Fat?'

She stands for a moment with the light behind her. She is about as far away from fat as there is to be. She is tall and thin boned. Her brown hair is pulled back from her face in a braid, showing off her hazel eyes. Her long, tan-coloured dress seems to be glued to her.

'You look so good.'

Fatima laughs and comes in to sit beside me, nimbly wrapping the skirt of her dress around her legs. She winces as she puts her hands into her lap, her brand obviously still hurting too, though her face shines with excitement. I suddenly realise she's also been told who her Chosen is. In my self-obsession, I had completely forgotten.

'Well?' She knows what I'm referring to.

'Titus.' She is still grinning. The branding must have done something to her brain.

'Titus?'

Fatima's face drops. 'I am ... happy about it.'

'Oh, okay.' I don't know what else to say.

'Pan, we have talked about the choices. Well, what there are of them ... Christophe? Or Thomas or Theseus?'

Yes, we have talked about Fatima's choices, skilfully avoiding talking about my options because she'd assumed, like everyone, I would be happy with Matthew as my Chosen. We thought Fatima would be paired with Christophe, Matthew's younger brother. He is of the same ilk as Matthew: dependable, solid, likely to be a good provider. Fatima had spoken of Christophe's good qualities, though, I have to admit, without much enthusiasm.

Thomas and Theseus, the twin sons of Hildur, were born before The Burning. Their father had ghosted not long after their arrival in the village and they were generally tolerated, even as they hardly worked and drank far too much root-juice. No one truly expected them to be chosen for anyone. I'd always assumed Titus would be paired with Emmaline, even if they are first cousins. Or, I hate to admit, Titus might have been chosen for me. He was, after all, another option apart from Matthew and maybe there was something appealing about his total arrogance and indifference to our existence. But, then again …

'Do you actually *like* him?'

Fatima looks down at her hands. I suspect she's about to cry. It wouldn't be the first time my questions have pushed her to tears and, though I hate myself for knowing it, probably won't be the last. We are best friends, but we also drive each other mad.

'He is really good looking,' she says in a small voice. Fatima is not like me. She doesn't have the imagination to picture what it might be like to spend every night of your life with a boy you have no emotional connection to, but who happens to be really good looking. I've never been able to talk about why I didn't want to be paired with Matthew. But too many times recently I've tried to picture my days with him in the future, to copy the way my mother's shoulders lift when she sees my father, the unconscious way she runs her fingers through her hair when they talk, the gentle way she places her hand on the back of his neck when he is tired. These images won't come. All I can see is myself flinching if Matthew tried to reach for me in any kind of romantic way.

'I think I can make it work,' Fatima's voice is stronger now. 'Titus and I just need to …'

'… Have an actual conversation?'

'You are not helping, Pan!'

'I'm sorry! I just don't understand why your parents have made this decision for you.'

'Well, they have. And, for the good of the village, we have to do what is expected of us.'

I look at her. She glares back. Whatever tears

she might have shed have been pushed aside by a determination I haven't seen before.

She stands.

'Today is all about becoming an adult, Pan. Maybe it is time you grew up.'

I watch her stalk out, trying to maintain her defiant posture even as she trips on the hem of her dress and pulls the skin hard against her branded shoulder. She cries out in pain.

'Fat, please ...'

She continues through the opening, holding her hand against the wound.

I can't lie here any longer. I hate fighting with Fatima. I hate this day. Although I know it's forbidden – part of our Blossoming is to spend time alone in our huts meditating on our future – I head out along River Road. I pass three huts, the same river-mud-brick domes as ours, each with a round hole in its centre to channel out our fire's fumes, and automatically name the inhabitants as I go: LeeYin and Barone, mother and father of Freya and Fee; and Eva and Stratum, parents of Hope. Across the way, the home of Atticus and Corrine, Titus's parents. I could go on and name all sixty of us. Everyone I have known since the day I, or they, were born.

Soon enough, I'm free of the huts, following the thin path through the forest. The trees are full of rustling sounds, the sunlight plays with their shadows and I start to feel as if I can breathe again, though the dress is more annoying than I'd imagined. It gets caught on low-hanging branches and, like Fatima, I find myself tripping on its hem.

When I emerge onto the stream's edge, it is alive with sparkles. The small fall that edges the pool keeps the water flowing but I still try to catch at my reflection, to see if the Blossoming has made any difference: no, my dark brown eyes, deep brown skin and short black hair all look the same. I want to look into the water and see a different kind of face. I'm not what they call pretty, nor beautiful. I have heard these words applied to Fatima and to Emmaline. The most I've been given is 'striking', my high cheek bones and thick nose enough to make me distinctive, just not in the way I want.

A large, brown bird flies high above, its wings spread out like two arrows. Such a sight is rare and I feel my heart pump. I know it is an eagle, one of the few birds left now. Perhaps this is a sign? A premonition of what's to come for me? Freedom, instead of entrapment? I'm not supposed to be superstitious, my father lectures me about staying firmly in the 'physical reality of my life', but I can't help it. Surely I can look for something to guide me, other than my parents? Surely my world could be more than what they decided in the Blossoming?

Finally, I get to do what I have been longing for all day, throwing off the dress and striding naked into the cool water. When I'm up to my waist, I dive in. The burn on my shoulder has lost most of its heat now, and the river soothes it more. As I stroke underwater I still feel pain, but it's becoming just another part of me.

I come up for air in the middle of the pool and float on my back. The sky above is pale blue, with wispy clouds running across it. Soon, the rains and storms will be coming and we will go for cycles of the moon without fresh bread. I don't want to think of the hunger ahead. I dive back down.

I run my hands over the river stones, thick with slime, at the bottom of the bed. I pick up a small one, so deep green as to be almost black, smooth with a hairline crack down its centre, just like the line in our hut. I seem to like things which look as if they're about to break apart. Maybe because I long for the shift this would bring to my life. I swim back to the surface.

As soon as I emerge, I can feel something is different.

On the opposite shore from where I came from, a boy stands. A boy? A man? He is only wearing pants, made from a skin I don't recognise, his chest and feet bare, though he is armed. Slung over his shoulder is a bow and a wooden quiver of arrows sits on his back. Around his waist is a knife in a sheath. I know of these weapons because I've seen them before, years ago when the Mountain People visited us. He's one of them.

He turns to look at me. There are black streaks of ochre under his brown eyes, a sign he is hunting. I paddle on the surface of the river, suddenly aware of how the crystal clear water doesn't hide me.

The man – I realise he's at least six notches on the Growing Tree older than me so I can't really call him a boy – doesn't hide his appraisal of my nakedness. I do not take my eyes off him either, determined not to be ashamed. There's a tiny smile on his lips, small enough to be missed if I wasn't watching so closely. My heart starts pumping and a hot tingling passes through me.

I open my mouth to say something, to break the spell that seems to have fallen upon me. He puts his finger to his lips, telling me to be silent. He tilts his head to the left, indicating a spot further up the river.

I look. There is nothing. Why has he told me to be quiet? Who does he think he is?

The hunter is kneeling now, hiding himself behind a large boulder. We wait, my arms and legs getting tired from staying afloat, paddling silently under the water. Finally, I understand the need for quiet.

A large cat – a cougar – slinks out of the forest. Crouching down to drink, its light brown fur blends beautifully with the sand of the river bed and the only sound is the lap, lap, lap of its pink tongue.

I should be afraid. I should be terrified. Such animals are one of the reasons for our boundaries, though this is my first encounter with one. But I don't feel scared. Maybe it's the novelty of seeing such a unique beast, maybe it's the presence of the boy, or maybe I've always wanted this danger ...

The hunter slowly takes an arrow out of his quiver and quietly fits it into his bow. Only gradually, as he stands up and begins to creep up over the boulder, do I understand I am about to witness this creature being killed.

I've seen goateeps have their throats cut; we eat their meat on special occasions and use their skins. I know there's no real difference between shooting this magnificent thing and slaughtering a goateep.

But I can't let it happen. Not today.

In my hand is the stone I took from the bottom of the river, clutched in my palm under the water's surface.

The hunter reaches the top of the boulder, lifts his bow and aims at the cougar's heart.

I kick myself up and out of the river and throw the stone as hard as I can towards the animal. The rock splashes loudly into the water, just near the big cat's mouth. The beast tenses, then looks up, snarling at the boy on the boulder. For a moment, I think it's going to jump up and attack him. Instead it turns, and bounds into the forest, massive legs pushing away through the undergrowth.

The hunter lowers his bow.

I swim back to my side of the river, walking out of the water to my dress, slipping it over my head and turning back around. The hunter looks at me now, although I don't know how long he's been watching me.

For a moment, I think he's going to shout across the distance, demand to know why I've ruined his hunt. His face looks hard and unforgiving. But he jumps down off the rock and makes his way along the bank to where the cougar was drinking. He reaches into the water and grabs something with his hand.

When he stands up, he tosses it up into the air and catches it in his palm: the cracked river stone I threw. He turns and runs into the forest, following the cougar's trail.

2

I walk slowly back to the village. Every part of my body feels alive.

I expect my parents to be in our hut and I dread having to make up a lie about where I've been. Only when I enter, it's not my mother and father waiting, but Matthew. He sits on one of our log seats, perched like a bird. I don't look closely at him, I'm too embarrassed. It's not as if I don't know exactly what expression he'll be wearing, exactly how his pale green eyes will be shining, like they always do when he's happy. On his head is the wide-brimmed hat we wove from river reeds. He has to wear it almost all the time, his skin is white and easily burnt. Despite the Blossoming, he stills wear the same clothes, goateep-skin pants and a loose vest. He stands up and takes off the hat. His white blonde hair is flat and he does his usual move of ruffling it up with his fingers.

Matthew was born soon after me and my parents knew his parents before The Burning. He is the kindest person I know.

'Have you been to the stream?'

I touch my damp hair and nod.

'Are you all right, Pan?'

I don't want to answer that question and wonder if the tingling in me is showing on the surface. I make myself busy stoking the fire back into life, listening to the quiet outside.

'Where is everyone?' I ask.

'That's what I came to ask you,' Matthew says. 'I thought my father would be back by now. I didn't want to risk going to the Great Hall. We're supposed to stay in our huts and wait, I know. But for how long? All the ceremonies should be done by now and our parents are supposed to be collecting us to join them. The sun will be going down soon.'

'Maybe the root-juice has gone to their heads.' Most of the village rarely drinks, so it wouldn't surprise me if the toast they make after the Blossoming had resulted in some forgetfulness.

I listen again to the silence outside. It seems different from before, as if I can feel something bad in the air.

Then a shrieking call: 'Titus! Pan! Matthew! Someone, help!'

Matthew and I look at one another. It sounds like Emmaline, although I can't remember hearing such panic in her voice before. I bunch up my dress and run out of our hut, Matthew following. We are not close to the hall, but Emmaline is still calling for us when we arrive, panting.

Emmaline stands at the opening of the Great Hall. She looks like she is going to be sick. Her normally immaculate blonde hair is a mess and there are streaks down her face where tears have fallen.

'Emmaline? What is it?'

She shakes her head, barely seeming to see me.

'There's something wrong ... with everyone.'

I look to Matthew.

'What do you mean?' he asks gently.

The gentleness seems to make Emmaline crack. She begins to sob.

'I came back because it was getting so late. And when I went in ... Go and see.'

She moves aside. Matthew and I slip into the darkened hall. For a moment, I think Emmaline has got it wrong: the adults have just got ridiculously drunk on root-juice, all of them lying on the ground, their cups spilling liquid everywhere. But then the smell hits me. The stink of faeces and vomit, meals of bread and goateep thrown up.

Matthew and I walk down the path we have both separately traversed early today. Now we walk in unison and with a different kind of nervousness.

'What's happened?' Matthew whispers, as if speaking any louder will make the scene come true, transforming it from the nightmare it surely has to be, into reality.

Lying across the path is Hildur, Thomas and Theseus's mother. I know, immediately, she is dead. A short woman, her body is contorted into a small ball, folding in on itself. I look down at her twisted face and feel some kind of shift, as if I'm going to leave the earth, as if something is going to take me.

I shake the feeling off as a horrible idea hits me. Why would I have believed they would not be part of this, even though the evidence speaks for itself?

I scream out: 'Mother! Father! Zaana?'

Jumping over Hildur, I try to remember where they would be, where their seats would be. Behind me, I hear Matthew calling for his father and brother, then Fatima's screams, trying to locate her parents and Cassie. Then Titus's deep voice booming out for his parents.

'Pan? Pan!'

My mother sits up against a tree-stump, my father's head cradled in her lap. I have to weave through others to get to her, some of them reach up to me but I'm brutal, pushing them aside. I want my mother. I fall on my knees next to her.

I don't want to ask.

I have to ask.

'Is he ...?'

'No, no. *Thank the rivers*. He's sick, very sick. As are all the rest.'

'But Hildur is ... dead.'

'She must have had low resistance. It shouldn't kill that quickly.'

'What is it?'

'I think it's an illness from the days before The Burning. I don't know how it's come back.'

I can't remember a time when my mother has spoken of The Burning. Whenever I have asked, she has always cut me off, telling me not to focus on what was gone, only on the here and now.

'We have to get your father, and all of them, rehydrated. We must boil all the water before any of them are given anything more to drink.'

'Is the sickness in the water?'

'I think it's the root-juice, but I can't be sure. We'll have to be cautious until we can find out.'

She gently places my father's head on the ground. He moans and I put my hand on his forehead.

'I'm here, father,' I whisper.

'I should have come to get you, Pan,' my mother says. 'But … I couldn't leave him. I just couldn't.'

I understand her need to stay with him. I really do.

My mother organises Matthew and Titus to carry out Hildur and place her in one of the empty store huts. Matthew's father, Omar, is one of the few older adults who has not been taken sick, though Matthew's brother, Christophe, is not so lucky. He, like my father, is in a bad way. Theodore is very ill. Fatima's parents, Whisper and Bren, are both sick. Her sister is fine.

This is as much of an inventory as I get to take, cleaning up, rushing around to collect wood and rebuild the hall's great pit fire, collecting goateep skins and reed mats from the huts, clearing the place of seats to allow for the skins to be lain around, helping to move the ill onto these makeshift beds, and checking on my father. All the time wondering at the strength and level-headedness of my mother.

How does she seem to know what to do? As if she's done this all before?

By the time the sun has gone down, I've almost forgotten how our life used to be. It seems as if it has always been this fog of moving through the sick, giving small sips of cooled water, applying damp rags to their foreheads, holding bowls for the retching; or comforting the young ones crying for their mothers; or, most horrible of all, helping Matthew to dig a grave for Hildur.

The Blossoming seems like a life-time ago, I don't even feel the pain in my shoulder anymore, and my meeting with the man and the cougar has become a distant memory. If I allow myself to think of it for even a moment, I feel guilty. My village is on the brink of ruin and I cannot indulge in Blossom fantasy.

Still, as the days go by in this way, I sometimes use my hunter's face to soothe myself to sleep, to replace the sight of my father clutching his stomach in pain or Christophe frothing at the mouth or Whisper digging her nails into my wrist and asking for more water. I feel so helpless. And I know I have to sleep or else I'll be too tired to keep going.

In my dozing, my hunter is throwing the river stone into the air and catching it again, his hand encircling what had once been in mine. He turns to run free into the dark, and many times as I remember that moment, I wonder what would have happened if I'd followed him.

3

'There is only so much I can do,' my mother says.

We are gathered outside the Great Hall, sitting in a circle on tree stumps: my mother, Omar, Rama, Matthew, Titus, Fatima and myself. We are the adults – as well as Davern and Cassie who are tending the sick – currently immune to what my mother has simply named 'the disease'. In the last week, we have lost another two more village members: Hamish, partner of Jeremiah; and Eva, the mother of Hope.

I don't want to admit how thankful I am to be away from the hall. This is the first chance I've had in a while to be outside, in the clear air, under the deep blue sky. I have to resist the urge to throw back my head and suck in a mouthful of coolness, free of sickness and worry.

'Will they die, Zaana?' Omar asks, pulling me back to earth, to the scary reality of what is happening.

Omar is what Matthew will look like in the future. His white hair matches his skin, his green eyes faded to a watery milk colour. He has the same gentleness. He doesn't look at my mother when he asks the question, his eyes cast downward. I am almost used to everyone addressing my mother as if she's the wisest of us all, in the same tone they once used for Theodore.

'Yes, they will die, eventually. They all have different levels of resistance. This is a strand of a virus which most of them can fight for a time, if we continue to care for them. But ... we need ...' my mother speaks quietly. 'We need ...'

'We need what?' Titus demands. I try not to notice Fatima wincing.

Titus's gold hair matches Emmaline's and I can't really remember him ever being anything but bare-chested. He is all muscle and confidence. But both his father *and* mother are lying in the hall next to my father, so I guess his aggression right now is understandable.

'We need a drug from the time before The Burning.'

No one speaks. In the silence are the ramifications of what my mother has just announced. Death for everyone infected – and, maybe, for those of us who haven't been infected yet, because we still cannot be sure of the cause of it – unless we do the impossible: travel to the city, Melney, and find this drug.

'What kind of drug?' Matthew asks. 'There were so many diseases ravaging the population before The Burning. If there were drugs to cure them, why weren't they used? We were told antibiotics were no longer effective.' He's always paid the most attention during lessons.

'It was … in development when I left.' My mother blushes. She clearly knows more than she's willing to talk about. 'It was being stored in hospitals, in laboratories, in preparation for use when … things turned around …'

'No one has been to the city since …' Rama doesn't finish her sentence, catching my mother's hesitation. 'We can't possibly risk it.'

'No, we can't,' Omar says, his voice deep and sad. 'We are truly at our end.'

He hangs his head, as does Matthew. The others seem to be gazing at nothing in particular. Are they really this willing to lie down and die? To not even try to save us? My heart beats faster, thinking of what has to be done, of where my next words might take me.

'I will go.' I try to make my voice sound confident, but it catches a little in my throat.

The circle turns to look at me, only slowly comprehending what I'm suggesting. Omar goes to speak and stops, his mouth half open. My mother shakes her head.

'No, no. That's not what I meant. Pan, there is no way I will let you.'

'There is no other solution, Zaana.' I use my mother's name deliberately, separating myself from being just her daughter. 'You have to stay here and lead the village. Someone needs to go to the city and find this treatment.'

I'm pleased with myself for using this word from our lessons, it makes me sound serious. Even as I say the words I hardly believe this is real, cannot imagine myself passing the boundaries, entering a world I've never seen before. But I will do it. If it means saving my father. If it means saving us all.

'You cannot go alone.'

Matthew's gaze leaves the ground and meets mine. My stomach does a flip. I have never seen him look so strong. And, although I never thought I'd feel this way, the idea of him coming with me brings a wave of relief.

'I'm coming too,' Titus's deep voice booms into the circle. 'I'm no good at all this nursing. I need to be doing something.'

In the corner of my eyes I see Fatima fidgeting. I hope she isn't going to say what I think she is going to say. Surely, she doesn't want to leave the village? Surely, she will stay with her sister? But, then, I know she has this dedication to making things work with Titus.

'Then I need to come too,' Fatima declares.

I suppress my groan.

'Are you sure?' I ask Fatima quietly, giving her the chance to change her mind.

She nods.

'Okay,' I say in as strong a voice as I can manage. 'We leave tomorrow morning.'

I know it makes sense for more of us to go, the logic of safety in numbers, the unspoken reasoning of not placing our hopes on one or two of us, the silent acknowledgement we might not all survive. But this is also why I'm not sure about Titus and Fatima coming. If this is all my idea, am I responsible for what might happen to them? What if they don't come back?

I can't really let myself imagine what we might face. If I focus on it too long, I know I won't be able to step one foot past the boundaries, let alone travel all the way to Melney. This is the place our parents fled twenty years ago and, in all that time, they have never gone back. What remnants we have with us – some clothes and books, items of steel like knives and scissors – are what were selected by the founding couples, Theodore and Tareen and Atticus and Corrine. For as long as I can remember, the city has hardly been spoken of: a taboo space where who-knew-what might lurk. I try to push it to the back of my mind, concentrating on what I should take, on the practicalities of leaving the village at the next rise of the sun.

4

My father had told me, in whispered conversations after my mother has fallen asleep, of how there were many, many, many people before The Burning. We had once been called The Great Southern Land, until the waters rose and we were no longer great and the continents shifted and we were no longer south. So we became simply the land, names were no longer important in our isolation. He once used the word 'thousands' to describe how many people there were but when he saw the confusion on my face, he changed it to 'many, many, many'. The use of the word three times made me think of our village with three times the amount of us. I know this is not nearly enough, but I find it hard to imagine such abundance. To think of having so many people who you didn't know, who you'd never seen or spoken to, whose family you hadn't sat down and eaten dinner with. It's kind of impossible to get my head around. And, also, kind of wonderful. Imagine having all those options ... Since I've known of the possibility, I have dreamt of it, of finding some other place out there, with more survivors. The many, many, many.

So now is my chance. To leave everything I have ever known and go into a world I have never seen. Not just ducking over the boundaries to swim in the stream, actually crossing the waters and plunging into the dark forest.

And I am completely terrified.

I cut my dress short, just below the knee, using one of the precious steel scissors we keep only for making clothes. I couldn't stand the thought of tripping over the dress and making a fool of myself in front of Titus and the others. Besides, it had occurred to me neither he, nor Matthew, changed their clothing during the Blossoming. So why should I put up with the foolishness of a long dress just because I'm supposedly now a woman? No matter what the ceremony was supposed to signal, I still feel like a girl.

I sit in our hut, alone, watching the fire. My mother is still at the hall and a part of me knows I should be there too, helping out for the last time. She insisted, though, I come back here and rest. 'Gather your strength', as she called it.

My strength. Do I really have any? I try to think of a moment when I've shown strength, when I've been required to show bravery or courage. Nothing comes. My life so far has been day after day of routines, of fitting into the village schedule. Familiarity has been the backbone of my years. How hard will it be without it?

Growing up with the River People, I have never been allowed to think of myself as anything out of the ordinary. We have a mantra, which begins every weekly meeting: 'We are not special. We are just survivors.' Theodore believes it isn't healthy to think of ourselves as lucky or selected. Pure chance has let us live. We do not name ourselves as anything other than those who dwell beside the river, a body of water we rely on without claiming it as our own.

So, I don't have any way of knowing how I will be if I'm tested. During the Blossoming, yes, I withstood the branding. But so did Matthew and Titus and Fatima and … Emmaline? I haven't had a chance to talk to her about her Blossoming. Poor Emmaline. She hasn't been helping out in the hall. Titus reported she was in total shock, lying in her hut, unwilling to move or speak. I've never been as close to Emmaline as I have to Fatima – we have totally forgotten our fight and have been giving each other support all during these days – and I've always felt bad about it.

'I thought you'd be asleep by now.'

My mother stands in the opening. The shadows from the fire make her face look even more tired and gaunt.

I hand her a bowl of soup I have been keeping warm by the fire. She takes small sips, sitting next to me on the ground.

'Who is doing the night shift?'

'Omar and Rama.'

'It'll be even harder when there are four fewer of us … I'm sorry, Mother.'

'You know I don't want you to do this, Pan.'

'I know.'

My mother hadn't argued verbally as much as I'd expected at the meeting. Her opposition just radiated out of her. There's no point in returning to it, though. She knows my mind is made up.

'*Why* are you doing this?' she asks and takes another sip of her soup, watching me over the lip of the bowl.

'To save us.'

'Is that the only reason you want to go?'

I can't tell her about my longings to see beyond the boundaries. She wouldn't understand. Those who leave, who ghost, are talked about as fools. Besides, I have my own questions.

'How do you know how to deal with all this, mother? You always said you were a manager in the days before The Burning.'

She's never given me more than this, using some lame joke about 'managing to get out of there' to deflect further questions. She drinks the last of the soup and places the bowl in her crossed legs.

'I lied,' she finally says. 'I was a doctor.'

I blink, hardly able to take this in.

'Like Theodore used to be?' I'm trying to find a reference point. We don't really have professions anymore and I only have a vague idea of what these words mean.

'No, he was a different kind of doctor. For the mind. I was for the body.'

'Then why ...?'

Why hadn't she has ever tended to those who've fallen sick before, from spider bites or colds and fevers? Why has she never even sat by me during the times I was ill? Always my father, rubbing my aching bones.

I stay silent. I don't want to accuse her, not with everything she's doing now.

'Many things happened, in the days before ...' her throat catches. 'I'm no longer a doctor.'

'But you are! You're saving us all.'

'What I'm doing is what anyone with any sense would do, Pan. Nothing more, nothing less. If you manage to find the drug, we might be able to save more of them, but that won't be thanks to any specialness of mine!'

I don't understand why she's angry with me. I don't understand her at all. She has never let me get close to her and, even now, with all that is happening, she won't tell me the truth about her life before. I feel tears scratching at the back of my eyes which I desperately don't want her to see. I suddenly feel too tired for this fight.

'I should go to sleep,' I say.

I lie down on my reed mat, with my back to her. I know this is a mean way to behave the night before I leave. I don't care. I do care. How can she have lied to me my whole life?

'I'm sorry, Pan. I didn't want to ...'

I feel her hand on top of my head. I close my eyes and hear her move away and lie down on her own mat, the one she usually shares with my father.

'I love you, Pandora,' she whispers.

I don't say anything, pretending I am already asleep.

In the morning, my mother and I walk to the Great Hall. She talks to me about the practicalities of the drug, telling me its name, describing its colour and the type of vials it will be contained in. Her voice is hard as she instructs me on how to use a needle to inject the medicine.

'You'll need to find a vein, the blue under the skin.' She sticks out her arm and I look at the river-like lines she is pointing to.

'But ... you'll be here, to do that ...' I say.

'We cannot know the future, Pan.' She sounds distant, as if she's already said goodbye to me.

Matthew, Titus and Fatima are waiting, each with a small skin bag at their feet, the same as the one I carry. Matthew wears his hat. Fatima is wearing her tan dress but, like me, she has cut it short. Titus stands, looking into the distance. I wonder what he feels for Fatima, whether he was as shocked as I was to hear the decision. There hasn't been time to dwell on this stuff and I can understand if his parents' survival has become his only concern now. I look at Matthew. We haven't had time to talk about our pairing either. I hate what has happened, but it has saved me from having to deal with *that* part of my life for a while.

Omar emerges from the hall and shakes hands with Matthew.

My mother hugs me. I cling to her as long as I can but I can't find any words to make it good between us.

Cassie hugs Fatima.

There's no one to farewell Titus.

We pick up our bags and begin to walk along the path named the Dead End. I am at the front, with Matthew only one step behind me. The sun shines as we leave the village – and everything we have ever known – behind us.

The path does come to a dead end, but we know to press on through the forest towards the river. Omar and my mother have talked us through it. We just have to follow the river west, then south and we will eventually come to the harbour of the city, though neither of them could really give us a sense of how long this might take.

'It wasn't a time for counting days,' Omar admitted. 'We just kept on walking.'

This was the closest Matthew and I have come to hearing about the immediate days after The Burning for our parents. Rama has always been willing to discuss the time long before – the different countries, different food, the languages spoken, and the 'technology' which died – but Omar, like my mother, wasn't fond of speaking about this part of their past. I guess they wanted to erase it from their memories, that strange dark period when they thought they could be the last, and only ones, left alive.

As we walk along the river bank, I wonder at this forgetting. The sandy edges are gentle on my bare feet and when I get hot, I stop and cup water in my hands, splashing the coolness onto my face. The forest on our left is exactly like the woods surrounding the village: patches of juvenile pines with thin, scrappy trunks (Rama says they are only about thirty years old and are the remnants of attempts at cultivation) mixed with naturally occurring oaks, their spreading branches providing sporadic shade. In the undergrowth, the occasional scurry of a rabrat, in the air the buzz of flies, and all around the sweet smell of the weed-flower, the small, pink star with a yellow middle growing in clumps along the bank.

My fear drops away for the briefest of moments, the beauty taking hold of me.

'It isn't going to be like this the whole way, Pan,' Matthew says, overtaking me. I've slowed down in my distraction. He stalks ahead.

I know he is probably right, but I have to try to be positive. This is the beginning of a journey that will save everyone. We are moving towards the place of all our hopes and maybe the land around us is going to be kind.

But Matthew is so right. By afternoon, the river is lined with rocks and boulders which cut at our feet as we crawl and climb over them. We have to keep side-tracking into the woods, only to encounter an undergrowth of prickled bushes, horrible, curly tangles of thorny branches we have to push through or risk losing sight of the water. We force ourselves on for as long as possible. By sundown, we are scratched and bruised, grateful to have the excuse of approaching darkness to stop and rest.

'I'm too tired to help make the fire,' Fatima declares and throws herself on the ground of the clearing we've found. I know if I sit down, I won't be able to get up again and I start gathering wood.

'Then I guess you'll be having cold goateep.' It's the first time I've heard Titus speak to Fatima directly. His voice doesn't hold any affection.

Fatima pushes herself back up off the ground. She keeps her head down. She's on the verge of tears.

'I want to go home,' she mutters under her breath. The two boys, rolling a large log they've found into the middle of the clearing, can't hear.

I am sympathetic – I have had the same thought over and over during the terrible scrambles and the cuts of my skin – but this isn't the time for self-pity. We can't be the girls who couldn't handle a mildly rough time, who limp back to the village after only a day's journey, letting everyone down.

'It's too late for that, Fat. Come on, you can do it.' She joins me in picking up kindling.

Soon, we have a fire going and sit silently, eating bread and warmed meat. Fatima refuses to look at Titus.

I have slept outside of our hut during really hot nights, our village laying down mats in front of the Great Hall. I loved these times, with the soothing of the young ones by their mothers, songs spiralling up into the humid air.

Out here, without anything familiar surrounding me, the open sky, overrun with stars and illuminated by the three-quarter moon, scares me. Out here, the tiny pin-points of light are what my father meant by thousands: the many, many, many. They don't make me feel safe or comforted, though; they make me feel small and unimportant.

We all lie near the fire on the hard ground, but separately. Matthew hasn't tried to come close to me. He might be afraid I'll push him away and humiliate him. I don't even know how I would react. Right now, I wouldn't mind warm arms around me, no matter who they belonged to. He still hasn't tried to speak to me about the Blossoming and there were times today when he might have. Maybe he isn't as happy about me being his Chosen as I'd assumed? Maybe we'll never talk about our supposed future together and it will all be forgotten about completely? The idea should bring relief, but it doesn't.

When I finally fall asleep, I dream I am floating in the black spaces in the sky, dipping my fingers into the starlight.

I wake in the darkness, somehow aware there is someone else in the clearing. The fire has almost gone out, only embers remain, and the shadowed figure hangs back from it, knowing they will be given away by its glow. My heart hammers, trying not to imagine what kind of creatures might inhabit this unknown forest. I force myself to speak, not wanting to lie in wait for an attack.

'Who's there?'

I wish my voice sounded stronger, more threatening. I'm trembling and my words are too weak to wake the others.

'Ssssh, it's just me, Pan.'

The voice is instantly recognisable. She moves into the light of the dying fire and her face, though less full and without its usual toothy smile, is still beautiful, framed by her golden hair. Emmaline.

'What are you doing here?'

'I'm coming with you to the city.'

'Don't be silly.'

'I came out of it, Pan, just after you'd left. The shock just ... lifted off me and I knew I had to follow you. Help you.'

She rubs her hands together, then holds her palms over the last remnants of heat. How has she found her way to us? She must have travelled some of the way in the dark.

'My father taught me tracking skills, you know,' she answers my unasked question. 'I will be useful.'

I can't really argue with her. She has the same motivation as all of us.

'Besides,' she draws her face into the shadows again, 'I only have my father – if he dies, I'll have no one.'

She puts down her bag and begins to clear away debris and leaf litter to make a space to lie down.

'Goodnight, Pan. I'll see the others in the morning.'

It's hard to go back to sleep. How will it be with Emmaline around? Will she be the leader now? Will both the boys follow her without the questions they keep throwing at me? Why have I never really been her friend? Is it because of her looks or her position as Theodore's daughter or her innate ability to make me feel so young and pathetic compared to her? All three, I suppose.

Only when fatigue is pulling at me, when my brain is in the fog of almost-sleep, do I recall Emmaline's words 'if he dies, I'll have no one' and realise this must mean, during the final Blossoming performed on that horrible day, Theodore didn't choose anyone for her.

5

The next morning I try to smile and look as happy as Titus when he sees Emmaline has joined us. He and Matthew hug her without hesitation and I lamely explain how I'm not surprised because I woke up and saw her last night, my way of covering my lack of enthusiasm.

Fatima is almost as bad as me. Her forced smile is thin and she mutters something about being pleased to see Emmaline active, before busying herself with repacking her bag. I don't think she has anything to worry about in terms of Titus and Emmaline, to me they act pretty much like brother and sister, but it's not as if *I* can give Fatima lessons on not being jealous.

After breakfast – some dried, salted goateep meat tasting like desiccated dung – we start out again. Only this time, Titus and Emmaline lead the way.

Though they are not exactly verbose – none of our recent experiences have made us chatty – they speak to one another more in one hour than the four of us did all day yesterday.

In one of their moments, Titus points out the light on the water and Emmaline stops to gaze at it. She cups a lock of hair behind her ear. Out of the blue, she eloquently begins to recite:

'The shining of the water's waves,

The silence of our deep and brave,

Tossed amongst the world at last,

Dream, but not of wonders past,

We step upon new, fertile ground,

Lost, and yet, newly found.'

My fingernails dig into the palms of my hands. These are words I've learnt too, we all have: the first stanza of the village poem, composed by Theodore, though I would never be able to speak it like this.

'The Burning has come, we are not gone …'

Only when she breaks off do I realise Emmaline is crying. Titus places his hand on her shoulder. She shrugs him off and resumes walking.

'Survivors now, we stumble on,' I whisper, finishing the poem, swallowing my own tears.

The rest of the day passes in silence.

After four days, even I am tired of the water reflecting the sun onto my face and the constant trickle of the river. How soon the new and different becomes familiar and irritating.

Sometime on the third day we passed to the other side of the river, driven by the increasing difficulty of finding a way through the boulders and bushes. I'd pushed for this move, claiming the opposing bank was clearer, though I was probably motivated by thoughts of the cougar hunter. We are on *his* side now.

Despite my ulterior motive, the forest on this side is thinner and it's easier to follow the river close to the bank. We are in the shade and I don't have to worry about Matthew getting sunburnt or Fatima's sweating face. The trees are large pines: many years' worth of long green bristle-like leaves have fallen, turned brown and now cover the ground. They are positioned almost in lines and all is quiet inside.

We have run out of goateep meat so keep our eyes out for any edible berries or roots to dig up and cook at night. We still have plenty of bread, but I have no clue what we will do when this is gone.

In the distance, we have begun to glimpse the mountains, another obstacle none of us were prepared for. Omar and my mother didn't mention them, so maybe we've lost our way because of changing to the other side of the river ... I'm not going to admit it, though. I can only hope we might be able to avoid the mountains, somehow.

We continue to hardly talk. Fatima avoids Titus, even as he's always hovering near Emmaline. I avoid being alone with Matthew. Matthew seems to be happiest walking on his own. I'd imagined the five of us would actually discuss our plans, sometime along the way we'd crack these hard shells we seem to have placed around ourselves, but it hasn't happened yet.

When I get a chance to tell Fatima about Emmaline's lack of a Chosen, she can't find any explanation for it either.

'Why would Theodore do that? Did he fall sick before he came to it?'

'I thought of that. But there isn't any drinking during the Blossoming. And if my mother was right, it was the root-juice that gave them the virus.'

We are walking a fair distance back from the other three and, for a moment, we stop. I know I am back in our village and I suspect Fatima is too.

I think of my father. I try to picture him

miraculously well, sitting up and giving my mother one of his joy-filled smiles. They weren't a common occurrence. Those smiles only came when the day's work hadn't been too exhausting or the village meeting wrangling hadn't been too disheartening or my own mood and my mother's had been exactly in sync with his. There were enough memories of them, though. Laughter, water fights, a witty comment about his cooking skills and his whole face would come alive.

I don't try for my mother in the same way. Not only because a part of me is still angry with her for lying, but because I know I won't find similar memories. Smiles, yes. Laughter, no. Never anything to completely remove the sadness lying underneath, the layer of unhappiness she's always had. She had lied about who she was before The Burning. What else hasn't she told me? How can I make it better for her? If I come back from this journey, returning triumphantly with the drug – a heroine – will she be so proud all her past will, finally, be forgotten?

'Maybe Theodore thought no one was good enough for his daughter? Not even Titus?' Fatima has been thinking different thoughts.

'Maybe.'

'But we don't really have that luxury,' Fatima

goes on. 'Our small numbers require us to ... breed. That's what the Blossoming is about, after all: giving our couplings importance and reminding us of how central choosing a partner is to the continuing life of the village.'

Fatima sounds like a younger rendition of Theodore. She has always held to the belief that our leader knows best. My father has taught me to be more questioning, although even he has succumbed to the idea of the Chosen. I shiver, watching Matthew climb over a log, his hat flopping up and down.

'How do you think they're doing?' Fatima asks, her voice trembling. 'Do you think my parents are ...?'

Like all of us, I know Fatima has been trying not to dwell on what might be happening back at home. It's the only way we can keep on.

'I'm sure they're fine,' I say, trying to sound convincing. It's the only way I can keep on.

We start walking again.

We haven't been able to find a clearing in the new forest, so we head back to the river's edge and try to build a fire on the bank. The ground is too damp, though, and nothing takes hold.

We sit in a circle around the non-fire, focusing on the spot where the flames should be. Above us is the dark shadow of a huge boulder. It sits alone on its side, as if thrown by some great force which I suppose it was, sometime long ago. The night settles in.

'Great, more stale bread for dinner,' Fatima mutters.

I'm disappointed too because we'd managed to find some roots and I had been thinking about root soup all afternoon. We wouldn't have had the special herb my father adds to it, but it would have been something warm, something to take away the chill.

'This isn't about you, Fatima,' Titus replies, once again scathing to his supposed Chosen. 'You're not exactly suffering compared to others. Stop being so self-centred.'

In the darkness, it sounds so cruel and, although I have my problems with the way my friend is behaving, I can't let it pass.

'Don't talk to her like that, Titus.'

He jerks his head up. He must be looking at me, although his face is just one black mass.

'Like what?'

This isn't the conversation I want to be having.

'Like … you don't care.'

Fatima draws in a deep breath. I have opened up something which I know, suddenly, I shouldn't have.

Titus drops his head down again. He will speak the words – *I don't care* – and there will be no going back, for Fatima or for him. The silence is like no other I've felt on this trip, as if we're all tensed together, our one moment of unity.

In the moment before Titus opens his mouth, we hear the growl.

Because I have heard the sound before, I immediately know what creature is making it, and spot a silhouette crouched on top of the boulder. I don't know whether to run or stay perfectly still. The last time I saw a cougar, *it* was the hunted, not me.

Slowly, we all stand and Titus and Matthew, who have their backs to the rock, turn and edge away from the low rumble emitting from the creature's throat. In the crescent moonlight, I can just make out the shine of its eyes. It is so close, I swear I can smell the wet tang of its fur.

'Run!' Titus screams and, in that instant, I know it's the wrong thing to do. We won't be able to outpace the cat in the dark. We will stumble and be taken easily. But before I can say anything, Titus sprints into the shadows of the forest.

'No! Get a stick, stay together!'

I can feel the hesitation in the other three. Who to listen to? Who to trust?

Matthew grabs a solid branch from the abandoned fire and dashes to my side. Emmaline quickly finds a weapon and pushes up next to Matthew. I too have a stick in my hand, though I have no memory of picking one up. The three of us huddle together, waiting.

Fatima doesn't move. She seems to be fixed on the spot where Titus abandoned us. Alone and untethered, she looks like an easy target, just one spring away from the great cat.

From the forest, a crashing sound. Titus must be coming back, reversing his decision to flee.

When I remember it later, and I try to remember it many times, I can't quite picture how it all happens.

It is just a mess, a flash of sounds and pictures: the cougar springs up, launching itself at Fatima, a figure emerges from the trees, the twangs of a bow, one after another, Fatima screams, the creature's gaping mouth, arrows flying through the air, I launch myself towards Fatima, the thud of her body hitting the ground beneath me, a strange moan, the stink of the large cat's breath, the pain of claws in my skin.

And then, stillness.

6

The stillness doesn't last. A cacophony of voices.

'What are the Babblers doing here? Where's their fire?'

'Pan! Pan!'

'Are they alive?'

'Is it dead?'

The last blood of the cat is running warm through its body. I can feel it on top of me, the final surge of its life force, I know it will not move again. It is at its end, no more time left in this world. Even as I realise this death has saved me, has saved Fatima, I feel a great sadness and I do not want to wiggle free, do not want to escape this strange cave of fur and teeth and claws. The creature is one with me, as long and swift as I am, and if I do not move, I will take on its soul.

'Get it off her! Help me get it off her!'

Matthew's panicked voice cuts through all the

others and there is straining and grunting and the body of the cougar is lifted away. I am released. I roll onto my back and open my eyes. My heart is pounding so hard, I can barely breathe. Matthew kneels beside me, looking down, his face crunched up with worry.

'Pan?'

I don't want to see him, I want to see the stars, I want to push him aside and dive up into the blackness between the twinkling fires of the sky, to join the cat's free spirit.

'Pan?'

'Leave her. Help me with the other one.'

I don't know this voice, but I feel its power. Matthew's face disappears and somewhere close by there is crying and hurt.

Above me, a star shoots across the darkness. I close my eyes and the line of fire in the sky is on the back of my lids. I am a streak across the night, soaring and then plummeting. I am tossed, I am held. This is an ending, and yet a beginning.

I am nothing and I am everything. I float in the darkness between the stars.

I am the stars. I am the darkness.

I am me.

Bright lights flash, then dim. Another streak of light. I fall, a rush of wind against my face, my stomach churning.

Someone, something, catches me. I am lowered onto the soft, soft earth.

I open my eyes. A cave, lit by a fire. The flicker of the flames like the stars. He is sitting across from me. My hunter, smiling. Not the small grin after I threw the river stone and made him run. A large, wonderful smile, his eyes shining with it. He reaches out and touches my cheek. I feel the heat of his fingertips on my skin. I see myself in his eyes, my star-touched face.

I shiver and, in the moment of my hesitation, he is transformed. I am no longer looking at his face. I am looking into the cougar's eyes. It snarls, its teeth bared and its breath hot. I close my eyes, waiting for the attack. I am not afraid, only sad this will be my ending.

Nothing happens.

Only the sound of the cat breathing and then a whisper: 'Kaplan'. I open my eyes and the cave is gone. I am the sky, looking down at all below me: the forest, my river and the mountains. And, in the distance, a shimmering, the light of the city ...

'She's waking up.'

I sit up. The sun is rising. Hours have passed. I don't remember sleeping. Have I been lying here all this time?

A fire is burning in a deep pit surrounded by river stones and, for a moment, I think I am back in the village; this could be one of our fire places, I could look up and see a cracked line running up to a chimney. Instead, there are faces, circled around. Some are familiar, some are not. I can't take them all in.

'How are you feeling, Pan?' A tentative enquiry from Matthew. He's sitting opposite me. Through the smoke his skin looks grey. Next to him, Fatima is lying on the ground, her eyes closed. Matthew has his hand on her head, gently stroking her hair. One of her cheeks is swollen and there's a gash on her forehead which seems to be coated in mud. Emmaline is seated at Fatima's feet, sitting on her heels. She is paying no attention to our wounded friend, though, her focus is on the figure next to me.

'You'll feel ... different ... for a while.'

This is the strong voice from before – how long ago was it now? only last night? – and I turn my head to see him sitting cross-legged next to me.

Him. My hunter.

He wears a fur cloak over his bare chest. Lying on the ground in front of him is the bow, and the quiver of arrows. He has one of the arrows in his hands, rubbing it with a piece of skin which, I notice, has dried blood on it.

Next to him is another one of the Mountain People. He too is in a cloak, though I think this is made out of rabrat skin and he has a vest beneath it, his body thin and weedy compared to the other. My hunter has thick black hair whilst the other is blonde with a sprinkling of freckles across the bridge of his nose. He looks to be only about fourteen notches on the Growing Tree. He has no weapons and glances enviously at the deadly projectiles at his companion's feet.

'Is she really a reader? A Babbler?' the younger one asks.

'Sssssh, Caro.'

He has used that word before – 'Babblers' – I remember it.

'Why do you call us Babblers?' I ask, my voice sounding strange after so much silence.

'*That* is your first question?'

The hunter smiles and shakes his head.

'Sorry, is there a better one?'

I feel the weight of everyone's attention, the way in which they are all watching me, wary. Only *he* seems relaxed, as if all of this is perfectly ordinary.

'I thought you were dead,' Matthew says petulantly. I focus again on Matthew's face through the smoke. His features are sharper now and I can't help looking at his hand on Fatima's head, my face growing hot at the intimate way he's touching her. I am not jealous. What is there to be jealous of? Yet, I don't understand why he is professing such concern for me whilst keeping such a distance.

'Sorry to disappoint.' I stand. The world spins.

'Whoa, take it easy.'

The hunter jumps up and grabs my arm with his hand, steadying me.

'You've been in a trance. You can't just skip out of it.'

The real heat of his palm on my skin is wonderful – it reminds me of his touch in my so-called 'trance' – but they are all there and I want to be alone, away from them: Matthew and his demands for my emotion, Fatima and her terrible wounds, Emmaline and her untouched beauty. A surge of nausea rushes up my throat.

'I'm going to be sick.' I break free from his grip and sprint into the forest. As I run, I catch a glimpse of the cougar's body, lying on its side as if sleeping.

I throw up three times, voiding all the bread and dried goateep meat of the last few days. Leaning over, I discover my entire chest is bruised and there are random scratches on my legs and arms. When I tentatively touch the shoulder blade where the brand is, my fingertips come away stained with blood from where claws have ripped my skin.

After I finish being sick, I sit at the base of one of the thin trees and wonder how I am going to face him again. What must he think of me? What kind of impression have I made? First, scaring away his kill, then throwing myself into the path of the cat. And, *then*, spacing out for hours. Not to mention, the awful questions and the disappearance to vomit ... I can't imagine walking back into the camp, showing my face again. Maybe I can just stay here until dark? Creep in when they are sleeping, wake up with them tomorrow as if none of this has happened?

Except, I know I have to go back. Deep inside my

'trance', there was something … a glimpse of what we need to know, a reminder of how we need to push on. I can't see it right now, it's like a shadow behind a boulder, only I know it is there, lingering. What was the word the cougar spoke?

A branch snaps and I startle, hoping to see my hunter appearing through the forest, coming to make sure I've recovered, full of concern. Once again, I'm wrong.

Titus appears from behind a bush, his shoulders slumped low. He coughs.

'I am so sorry,' he mutters. His eyes are red from crying. I have never seen anyone look so ashamed. Of all the people, I'd never expected Titus to act like a coward. Where has he been all this time? Has he really been too embarrassed to show his face again? I can't really blame him for running scared from the cougar. I might have done the same if I hadn't seen one so recently.

'It happened,' I say. I can't lie and say it was fine to do what he did. He could have got us killed.

'I guess my father was right. He always said I was all muscle and no brains.' I had never realised Atticus was this hard on him and feel guilty for thinking almost the same.

'We should go back to the others, Titus.'

'What will they think of me?' he asks, echoing my own thoughts.

I shrug. I have no idea what is going on in everyone else's minds. I can hardly figure out what's going on in mine.

Returning to the others with Titus does get me off the hook, though. All the attention is on him when we walk out of the forest.

'What are you doing here?' Matthew demands, striding towards us. I have never seen him look so angry. 'Do you think we want you back, when you've shown your true colours? Why don't you go slink back to the village and see whether you can do something useful there?'

'Calm down, Matthew,' I say.

Matthew is not done. He shoves Titus in the chest. 'Why should I calm down?'

Over Matthew's shoulder, I can see Fatima sitting up, her swollen cheek almost black. I can't spot Emmaline or the Mountain People.

'Who do you think you are? The big and mighty son of Atticus, always looking down at us, always making out you were better than us.' I've never heard

Matthew speak like this. I never realised he felt this way. 'Who's better now, hey? Who's the weak one now? Hey?'

He shoves Titus again. I think he expects Titus to resist. The son of Atticus has no fight left in him, though, he is in a mess, and stumbles backwards, almost falling.

'Stop it.' I speak quietly, hoping to cut through Matthew's rage.

'What kind of man runs away, leaving his women to die?'

I wonder if I could possibly have heard right. *His* women? This is the way Matthew thinks of us?

'Leave him alone!' Fatima is standing, with difficulty. Her weight is all on one leg, the other is bulging strangely at the ankle. She has probably broken a bone. She totters and we all race over to her, the fight forgotten in our need to stop her falling.

Titus gets there first and, putting his arm around her, helps to gently lower her to the ground.

'I'm so sorry,' Titus says again, this time to Fatima and then, again, to Matthew. 'I'm sorry.'

It is the softest I have ever heard him talk to either of them.

Matthew ignores him. He squats down next to Fatima.

'Are you all right?' he asks and she nods. He walks away to sit by the river. Titus stays on the ground with his arm around Fatima.

I squat down next to Fatima as well. I can't believe the state of her face. I realise she must have hit rock when I pushed her to the ground to protect her from the cougar.

'Are you really all right, Fat?' I ask.

'Yes, Panda, thanks to you.' I smile when she uses her nickname for me. Rama had told us about these big gentle black and white bears who happily chewed on the same plant all day. Fatima had said this sounded about as far away from me as it was possible to be and so, of course, started calling me it. 'My ankle hurts like crazy though.'

'Did you twist it?' Titus asks.

'Yes,' I see her glance at the arm Titus still has around her shoulder. I can tell she's pleased.

I'm embarrassed at how relieved I am when Emmaline returns by herself and, not long after, the two Mountain People emerge from a different part of the forest. I have washed myself in a bend of the river a little distance from the camp. The water ran red at first, the wounds on my shoulder reopening. I tried to rid myself of the layers of dirt and dust, tried to get my hair to look less like a matted clump on my head. I am trying to carry myself more like a woman and less like a young boy. Even as I do it, I dislike what I'm trying to do. This preening. What will it matter? He has already seen the difference between Emmaline and me – her 'beautiful' versus my 'striking' – and I've already seen the way she is looking at him. I can't compete.

Still, I feel that rush through my whole body when he comes up to the fire. I am not looking at him, intent on pushing embers around with the end of a stick, so I can hardly feel irritated when he doesn't actually speak to me.

'You must be Titus.'

'Yes.'

'I'm Bayat, and this is my tribesman, Caro. We call ourselves the Mayhaanan, after our leader.'

Bayat. Can I really give up thinking of him as anything other than my hunter?

'Thank you Bayat. From what I hear, we owe our lives to you.'

I can't help smiling at the formal way Titus is talking, as if he's speaking in a village meeting. My smile draws Bayat's attention and I raise my head to find him looking at me. He has the same small grin on his face I saw after he tossed the river stone into the air. His cheek bones stand out sharply against his dark brown skin.

'You look ... better,' he says.

This is the best he can do? As annoyed as I am at the efforts I have put in to making myself presentable, I am even more annoyed he's noticed them and, even worse, thinks they are worth mentioning. There's no good way to respond to this. I stay silent.

Somehow, he gets it.

'I mean ... you look as if you're *feeling* better. I hope?'

I can barely believe I've made him stumble.

'Yes, I am feeling better,' I reply. 'My name is Pandora.'

For some reason, I want to give him my whole name. And I want to say thank you, but I can't bring myself to. Not because I'm ungrateful, only that the words seem so inadequate. Thank you for saving me from certain death? Thank you for saving *us all* from certain death? I don't want to sound like Titus, as if this debt can be repaid with just words.

'Where have you put the cat's body?' I ask instead.

When I returned from the forest I noticed the cougar had gone and assumed the Mountain People had taken it to be buried.

His cheeks turn red, as if suddenly embarrassed.

'Over here!' The young boy, Caro, calls out. He is standing near the boulder the creature leapt from, his foot on top of something, a something which might once have been alive but is now a red, gory lump.

'No,' I say softly. I don't want to believe it.

'It is our way,' Bayat speaks just as softly, like he knows I don't want to hear. 'We don't hunt the great cat for fun. We use every part of it.'

He strokes his fur cloak, the pelt is light brown and smooth. I catch the whiff of blood on his hands.

I can't explain why I feel like crying. Why had I thought the animal would be treated any other way? Why does my stomach keep turning, twisting as badly as on the morning of the Blossoming? How can I be showing such silliness in front of the only person I've ever met who I desperately want to impress?

'You saved her once.' Bayat's voice continues to float over me. The others run to see the carcass, to rejoice in the meat they will now get to eat, to run their hands along the drying skin spread out on the rock. 'You gave her many more days of life. And she was grateful. She took you into the night sky and let you see ... You are a reader, Pandora ...'

'Bayat!' Caro calls. 'The Babblers have never seen anything like it!' He sounds so proud.

I close my eyes. My tears fall. The sadness of the cat's death seeps into me. When I open my eyes again, Bayat is gone, standing with the rest of them near the dead cougar.

What did he call me? A reader? I am hardly able to read the symbols Rama scratches into the dirt, the letters which link to the sounds we speak. It has to be another kind of reading, I suppose, the kind which takes you out of your body and far away from all you thought you knew.

'We call you Babblers because of the river.'

Caro chews on a large piece of meat. He and Bayat have prepared a piece of the cougar on a long, whittled spear which they've placed over the fire pit, held up by two forked branches driven into the ground. They have turned it sporadically over the course of the afternoon and then carved slices off it.

Matthew, Fatima, Titus and Emmaline took their offerings without question, obviously relishing the freshness of the flesh.

I took mine too, without looking Bayat in the eye,

but I haven't been able to bring myself to eat it. It sits next to me on the log I occupy, a little bit higher and a little bit away from the others and, in the meantime, I tear small bits of bread from the stale hunk I have left. I don't think anyone's noticed. They're too busy with their conversation.

'I don't understand.' Fatima's cheek has faded to purple and she is sitting up without wincing. Her ankle is not broken, only badly sprained. We are yet to discuss what she's going to do. In fact, no one seems willing to bring up the subject of what we are planning.

'The river babbles. You spend your time by the river. So, you are Babblers.'

'Oh, I see.'

'What do you call us?'

Caro's face is eager. He is clearly loving this adventure, a chance to capture stories he can tell to his friends back in the Mayhaanan tribe. Even though I am only a few notches of the Growing Tree more than him, I feel much, much older.

There is an awkward silence. None of us want to tell him the very uninteresting name we have ascribed to his kin.

'The Mountain People,' Fatima finally mumbles and Caro's expression falls.

'The Mountain People?' He repeats it with such disappointment, I have to hold back laughter. I don't want to offend him.

'But,' Fatima tries to explain, 'we call ourselves the River People. So, you see, we don't ... try very hard.'

This ridiculous apology sets me off again and I am giggling behind my hand. Caro whips his head around and catches me. He has a big smile on his face.

'Do you think it's funny, Pan?'

'Sorry, Caro.' I am laughing fully now, and the others begin to join in. 'We'll try to come up with something a bit more imaginative.'

'Peakers?'

'Mountaineers?'

'High-land Heroes?'

'Stoners?'

I lose track of who is suggesting what. It doesn't really matter. For the first time since we left the village, we are teasing one another and, for the first time, we are laughing. I feel a heavy weight lift off my shoulders. Maybe we are going to be all right.

LETTERS

1

To my daughter,

I have begged some precious paper from Rama to write to you in my rest time. Rama tried to insist this wasn't a way to rest, but I want to talk to you, Pan. Any way I can.

My heart has been whispering I might not see you again and this may be the only chance I have to explain … many things. I hope my heart is wrong. I hope you will not have to read these words, though I know my hopes have no control over what might happen. I have been foolish. There are so many things I couldn't, or wouldn't, tell you. And, now, it might be too late.

Where to begin?

It has been three days since you left, since you walked up the Dead End and disappeared from view. I hope you won't ever have to feel the way I did that morning; that your whole body will never feel the longing and ache of seeing someone you love go, and the pain of their decision not to look back at you. It's not that I blame you, Pan. Despite what you think, I do understand your desire to leave, your need to search for another kind of life. You were born into this village and haven't known anything else. I've seen it in your face, almost always: this need to find more. I do understand. But I'll come to that later.

After you, Matthew, Titus and Fatima left, we went back to nursing the sick. Within a few hours, we were lucky to see a great improvement in Christophe, Matthew's brother. He was suddenly sitting up and breathing normally. This gave us great hope and I had the notion of running off into the forest and commanding you to come back home. It would have been a mistake. None of the others have shown similar turnarounds although, at this point in time, we have not had any more deaths.

It was a great help to have Christophe well, as there are now six of us (including Cassie) to tend to the thirty-seven ill, as well as to look after the twelve young ones. I won't tell you what a surprise it was to discover Emmaline had gone, and a disappointment, as I had hoped for her assistance once her shock had passed. But there was nothing to be done about that.

We have organised the time into four different shifts: looking after the sick, small children care, crop and animal tending, and rest. How you would hate it! The days are almost completely the same, there is none of the variety which Theodore used to insist upon – he certainly did know how to keep people happy – and the hours do drag. Although it will seem strange to you, my favourite time is in the Great Hall, amongst the disease. Not only because it is the time I am able to spend with your father but because it brings back memories I have long suppressed and which might end up saving us.

I told you, Pan, I had been a doctor before The Burning. I know you could barely believe it because I so rarely tended to you, because I have never been there for all the smaller illnesses which have threatened us, because I have never admitted to it before. You have known Ravena as our midwife and Eva as our medic. With her death, I might have been forced to admit my former calling, although even before I knew of it, I sensed this would be the time when I would have to face my past. And so I will face it.

How can I paint you a picture of a world so completely different to your own?

You've been taught to think about The Burning

as one day when everything changed, when the final destruction came. Yes, there was that one day in Melney. But change comes gradually and more often when we aren't even looking, walking towards the end with our eyes closed. The land had lost so much and so many: climate refugees driven to the city as the only place where life seemed sustainable; outside a world of famine, sickness, pollution. Leaders who were corrupt and uncaring. Mass animal extinction. *These* were The Burning Days.

I lived in an apartment, a box piled on other boxes, high into the sky, with a man who was not your father. We had met during our studies in medicine. See? Even this will be a concept you can't understand. The idea of dedicating all your time to reading and learning. Your classes have always been short and sporadic, too many other things to be done, like growing and laughing and loving. The idea of becoming only one thing – a doctor or a lawyer or a vet – is completely foreign to you.

Okay, I need to get back to the point. I can hear your impatience, Pan, as if you were here in front of me, giving me one of your quizzical looks. I wish you knew how beautiful you are. Okay, okay. I'll get on with it and anything you don't understand, you'll just have to skip over.

The man who was not your father was called Ivan. He and I became a golden couple, graduating with top honours, and the world seemingly at our feet. The only problem was that the world was changing. I remember hearing your father talk to you of 'thousands' of people, forgetting to mention there had once been 'millions'. For so long, we over-populated, the globe barely coping with our numbers. But after we had destroyed so many biosystems, initiating the sixth extinction, we were finally reduced. Or, to be clearer, we reduced ourselves, with the Climate Wars, as they were called.

When I was born, we'd reached some kind of plateau, countries too exhausted to continue the fight. My parents, and Ivan's, were hopelessly optimistic and we trundled on, as if we could live the same kind of lives, with petrol at its end, with clean water a luxury, in a city still broken and bent from conflict. My parents had grown up through days of bombings, but it was almost more terrible when the bombings stopped, because it meant the rest of the world no longer cared about us.

My university days were, perhaps, the best of my life. When I look back now, I can't understand how naïve I was, how I couldn't see where we were headed, how shielded I was by my parents' money and their continued ability to buy their way through crisis after crisis: food shortages, electricity burnouts, poverty riots. I can't yet bring myself to tell you how your grandparents made their money in the first place, that will have to be another story.

The apartment Ivan and I moved into after graduating was part of a gated community and despite my desire to be in the hospitals which so sorely needed me, my parents arranged for me to work in a commercial research department. Again, I suspect you will have no idea what I'm talking about. Picture white walls, white tables and white coats. I am there also, white with fatigue and sadness. I would like to tell you I was working hard on a project to help the sick, to find cures for the many diseases which had continued to ravage the population, to turn around the animal die-out, breeding the hybrids that would save us. I would like to tell you I was noble and good, fighting for the survival of all.

I can't tell you this, Pan. I can't lie anymore.

Rama has just stuck her head into our hut to tell me it is my turn to milk the goateeps. It is past midday already. I must have paused longer between sentences than I realised. This is harder than I reckoned upon.

I will tell you more, Pan, when I am able to. Until then, stay safe.

Your loving mother,

Zaana

PART TWO

7

The moon is at its halfway point through its cycle: a slab of light in the night sky. I sit outside our cave with my legs crossed. I can barely believe we have been here five days already and I am thinking of the hole at my back as *our* cave, the one I've been sharing with Emmaline and Fatima.

In the distance, deep in the forest canopy, I hear the strangled bird shrieks I have almost become used to. Caro has told me they are screech owls but this sounds too strange, and I wonder if he has made it up. If there is anything I have learnt here, it's that Caro likes to tell stories. I don't want to admit how little else I have learned, especially about Bayat.

After the laughter died down that night, he asked

us, seriously, what we were doing out here and how we didn't know not to be in this place, after dark, without a fire. Before I could say anything, Emmaline began to explain. She talked in her smooth way, making our story sound like a poem. To give her credit, she did place me at the centre of the tale, emphasising how it was me who insisted we try to find the medicine in the city (I suppose Titus must have told her, since she wasn't actually there). Still, I couldn't help seeing how Bayat watched her, drawn into her web of words. The firelight danced across her face.

When she finished, my hunter looked over at me. I still had the meat of the cougar sitting on the log beside me, my fingers sticky from having touched it too often, even as I hadn't managed to actually pick it up yet. I'm not sure what I expected to see in Bayat's face. Maybe admiration? Or awe?

'Are you out of your mind?'

No, this wasn't what I'd hoped for: irritation and barely concealed contempt.

'The city is dangerous,' he continued. 'You're not even hunters. Do you know what's there? Have any of your people been back, since the End?'

This was, clearly, their name for The Burning.

'No,' I said. 'But this is the only way to save

them, so we'll just have to face ... whatever.'

'*Whatever?*'

'Why don't you tell us?' Matthew piped up. He looked irritated as well, I suspected for a different reason. 'Since you're obviously an expert.'

Bayat shook his head. He opened his mouth again, as if to begin a tirade, then closed it. He sighed.

'We all need some sleep.'

That night, as we lay around the fire, I tried to hear Bayat's breathing, to pick out his particular rhythm. I couldn't find it. I could hear Matthew, the tiny snores I'd got used to since we began our journey, a new knowledge of him. I thought of how scared Matthew sounded when he said he thought I was dead and the way he had cried my name just after the cougar pounced.

I fell asleep and dreamt my mother was calling for me to come home.

I'd expected Bayat to bring up the question of our going to the city in the morning. Instead, he said we would have to come and stay with his people, at least until Fatima's ankle was healed. I knew I should argue, that I should advocate for leaving Fatima behind as we pushed on. But my own body felt bruised and weak and I suspected the other three felt the same because nobody raised any objections.

We made a stretcher for Fatima out of Bayat's cloak and two long branches and took turns carrying each end. For whatever reason, my turns always coincided with Matthew's, the three of us trundling along in silence behind Emmaline, Titus, Bayat and Caro. The young boy was the one who talked the most. He re-told the story of the hunt: how Bayat had been tracking the cougar for so many moons and abandoned the chase to return to the tribe. How Caro had convinced him to go out again, with him. How proud his father will be to hear Caro was there, when she was caught at last. Bayat didn't say much during this recount, I couldn't tell if he was irritated or embarrassed.

Once we reached the rocky outcrops at the beginning of the mountains, the stretcher became impossible to manoeuvre. Titus carried Fatima on his back. She was quiet, even as I could see the pain on her face with every jarring movement.

Thankfully, there was a path to follow or, at least,

the way Bayat led us along the ravines and through the crevices made it feel like a path. I never saw him stumble or hesitate, even as we climbed higher and the way became steeper and harder. He moved as if he knew every footstep intimately, as if the rocks were another part of him.

The rest of us didn't do so well. Many times, we had to stop and help one another over the grey, lichen-covered boulders randomly thrown in our way, blocking the dirt ribbons threading through the land. We scratched our hands and feet all over again.

The air became thinner until all I could hear was the sound of my own panting. I watched as clouds of white flew from my mouth with every breath and my skin pimpled up from the cold. It wasn't like the cold of the river, it made me feel dry, even as sweat ran down my back and arms. Whenever Bayat turned to check on us, I kept my head down, knowing my face would be red and hideous.

We continued along a plateau. No trees or anything green. We had to be careful with every step, the ground was crumbly. There was so much mist we couldn't see anything below or above us and the view I had hoped for – looking down at our river from up high – was denied me.

When at last Bayat stopped on a circular ridge,

just before the sun was going to set, I thought we were going to have a break. He cupped his hands to his mouth and made the most startling sound: a roar, like a wild beast, echoing up into the sky. Just above us, I suddenly realised the rocks weren't solid; they were hollow, a series of holes. I counted six and stopped, because there were people coming out of them, nimbly jumping down the ledges. They ran to greet Caro and Bayat. I watched for a young woman to embrace my hunter tightly or, at least, a mother or father to clench him in relief. They all hugged him happily but none of them lingered.

The Mountain People had not experienced the sickness we described and Mayhaan, Caro's father and the leader of the tribe, a man with the thickest neck I have ever seen, wasn't particularly interested in helping us.

'I am pleased Caro's first hunting trip ended so well,' he said. 'To see a kill is a privilege, but leaving your village to travel to Melney is foolish and unwise. Your elders should have known better.'

'Most of our elders are gravely sick,' I replied, trying to be polite.

A fire blazed in a dug-out hollow in the stone ground upon which we sat. In the caves above, I could see other fires flickering. Most of the tribe – I guessed it was about the same size as our village – had come out to examine us, and to take their share of the cougar meat Bayat and Caro had carried with them. As night fell they had retreated back to their holes, their homes.

I knew I should have been more grateful. I was sitting, warmed by a fire with my belly full of soup made by Caro's mother, Bettina. Every part of my body was content except ... Bayat was sitting opposite from me, next to Emmaline. Matthew sat at my side and kept handing me fresh pieces of bread, even though I didn't need them. This was enough to drive me nuts. Having Mayhaan dismiss our plans just added to my frustration.

'What did you expect us to do?' I continued, trying to keep the anger out of my voice. 'Stay and watch them die?'

Mayhaan paused.

'Perhaps.'

Mayhaan's face was brown and wrinkled, his hair starkly white, sticking out in tufts from his head. I tried to remind myself of the respect I was supposed to feel for such figures. He was Theodore all over again, with the same knowing eyes and the same melodic voice.

'We aren't prepared to do that,' I said.

'You aren't prepared at all.' This from Bayat who, up until this point, had remained quiet.

Just before I had told the story of our coming. I knew I didn't do it as well as Emmaline but I needed to say it aloud, to try to make sense of what had happened so far.

'I asked her before if she knew what was in the city.' Bayat was speaking directly to Mayhaan, as if I wasn't there. 'She doesn't know. None of them know.'

Mayhaan frowned. 'This is not our battle, Bayat.'

'How do you know? How do you know the disease won't come to us? How do we know they haven't brought it with them already?'

Mayhaan stood suddenly. 'If you thought that was a possibility, why did you bring them here?'

I could barely keep up with the thoughts rushing through my head. Battle? Who did we need to fight? And surely if Bayat had thought we were sick, he wouldn't have brought us here? Risked his tribe?

Bayat slowly stood. My stomach clenched as he glanced at me.

'I ... I don't know why I brought them here.'

'We aren't sick,' I tried to reassure him.

'No, no, we aren't,' Matthew chimed in. He placed his hand on my knee, rubbing my skin with his thumb. Of all the times for him to be, finally, physical with me ...

'I just believe we have to help them.' Bayat spoke directly to Mayhaan, again as if no one else was there. A silence, as they squared off against one another. 'She is a reader.'

Mayhaan turned, staring down at me. 'You know this for sure?'

'I saw it.'

Another silence. Mayhaan gave a small shake of the head.

'It is not enough.'

He strode away. Bettina and Caro quickly followed him.

'What was that about?' Fatima asked. 'What's a reader?'

'Tomorrow,' Bayat spoke into the flames, ignoring Fatima's questions, 'I'll start training you.'

'Training us for what?' I asked.

'To survive.'

He glanced down at Matthew's hand on my knee, turned, and disappeared into the darkness.

8

'Pan? Are you awake? Pan?'

In my half-sleep, I hoped it would be Bayat, even as I knew, in my heart, it wasn't. I could just make out Matthew's shape against the grey light of pre-dawn, framed in the cave's opening. We had slept as far away from the opening as possible – and the cave was deep, hollowed out years before by hand – though you could still feel the winds.

Since we had left our village, I had longed, every night, for the cosiness of my family hut. Sleeping in the open had been bad and the cave was one step closer to that old life but, somehow, it made it feel even further away. The difference just reminded me of how everything had changed.

'Pan?'

I considered pretending to still be asleep, though immediately realised how cowardly this was. I sat up and crept over Emmaline and Fatima. I wondered if, they too, were feigning sleep and, therefore, decided I would speak with Matthew far away from their possibly listening ears.

'Yes, Matthew?'

'I need to talk to you.'

I nodded. I knew, the moment he placed his hand on my knee, we would have to have this conversation. So much had been delayed. My time had run out.

'Let's walk,' he said, a tone of command in his voice. So, this was how it was going to be, was it?

We took the path which, yesterday, we'd stumbled up together, though we hadn't known it to be the final push. I couldn't help thinking of Bayat, standing at the fork of the track and giving his astounding roar, as if the dead cougar had been reborn in him.

'Let's go a bit further,' Matthew insisted. Maybe he was remembering Bayat too and wanted to get as far away as possible from the memory. I was absolutely sure Matthew's sudden attention towards me came from jealousy.

The morning breeze was cold, patches of scrub dripped with dew. I rubbed at my arms, hoping to get the blood moving.

We came to a nest of boulders and squeezed into the circular space inside them. Sheltered from the gusts, I squatted down and waited. Matthew stayed standing.

'With all that has happened, Pan, I understand why we haven't had a chance to discuss our future.' He spoke as if he had rehearsed these words, over and over. He wasn't looking at me. He seemed to be talking to one of the stones. 'But we were Chosen for one another and, in the normal course of events, we would have already begun living our lives together.'

He didn't sound like himself. It was as if he had turned into his father or, worse, Theodore.

'Nothing is normal anymore, Matthew.' I didn't want to have an argument. I wanted to save my energy, to be ready for Bayat's training. 'The disease has made everything different.'

'No!' He squatted down and gazed intensely at me. 'Not everything has to be different. We have an obligation to ... the survival of our people. We have to do what is expected of us.'

'Expected?' I felt like I'd been stabbed. 'That's why it's important to you? That's why *I'm* important to you?'

If I had anticipated anything from Matthew, it wasn't this. At least he could've pretended it was about love.

'No, that's not what I meant.'

He tried to reach his hand out to my face. I couldn't let him. I stood at that moment and his arm fell to his side. I looked down at the top of his head, his hair flattened from all the time he wore his hat.

'I know you are my Chosen, Matthew, and I would never do anything to hurt my parents. Never. When we are back at the village and everyone is saved ... when we are back home ... I'll do what is expected of me. But, until then, I want things to stay as they are. Nothing ... more ... between us than there's ever been. Okay?'

He glanced up and I could see the hurt in his eyes. I didn't want to hurt him, only I had to be clear: I wasn't *his* woman. I wasn't anyone's.

When I got back, the tribe was awake. The large stone ridge upon which we'd sat last night seemed to be common ground and many families were sitting around the newly stoked fire, eating their breakfast. There seemed mainly to be small children and adults the same age as my parents, those who would've survived The Burning.

Fatima and Emmaline were sitting with Titus, each with a small wooden bowl and spoon in their hands. They were hunched over from the cold, despite the fact the sun was up and shining, and I wondered how we would cope with the iciness of the mountains. Or how we'd cope with all that was, apparently, coming.

'Are you okay, Panda?' Fatima asked. I must have had my inner storm on my face.

'Yeah, I'm fine.' I would have to talk to her later. I would have to find some time to finally tell her about Matthew and me.

A grey-haired woman came up and handed me the same kind of bowl and spoon as the others had. Her face was smooth, despite the colour of her hair which she wore in long plaits. The bowl was full of some kind of crushed nut mixed with what tasted like goateep's milk. I had not seen, or heard, any goateeps though – their bleating was constant background noise in our village – and I wondered what it was.

'When do you think we'll start?' Emmaline asked. I'd heard this question before and was taken back to the day of the Blossoming, when the five of us had stood outside the Great Hall, waiting for the ceremonies to begin. I closed my eyes and saw the circle and the three waves of my branding. I could sense them in my skin, as if they were deeper than before. I remembered my trance and the feeling I was in the sky. Perhaps there was more than just this 'physical reality'? Could I really read another world alongside our own? When I thought of my father lying sick and the dead already buried in the river dirt, I couldn't understand how this would help them.

'Pandora?'

I opened my eyes and found Bayat sitting in our circle. He was bare-chested again, without his fur cloak, and when I went to move, I found it was on my shoulders.

'You looked cold.'

I didn't feel him place it there – why hadn't I felt him place it there? – and couldn't think of what to say.

'No need to thank me,' he smiled.

'Oh, thank you,' I muttered. Why couldn't I get something as simple as that right?

'Where's Matthew?' Titus suddenly asked. I felt blood rush into my face. I knew Bayat was watching me, even as he pretended to concentrate on eating his breakfast.

'I don't know.' I tried to sound as casual as I could.

'He was up very early,' Emmaline smirked. 'You really should tell him to find a way to get your attention without having to wake us all up, Pan.'

My whole face was burning and if there'd been a chance to throw my bowl of nuts-and-whatever at Emmaline's head, I might've taken it. Luckily, or not, the subject of our speculation walked up.

'Matthew!' Fatima cried. 'We were just wondering where you were.'

His hat was back in place, covering his face in shadow.

'How is your ankle?' he asked Fatima. He didn't even glance at me.

'Getting better, thanks. Although I still won't be able to train with you. Whatever that means.' She giggled.

'When are we going to begin this so-called training?' Matthew asked Bayat, anger in his voice.

'After breakfast.'

'I'm not hungry.'

'Okay.' Bayat put down his empty bowl. 'Then now, I guess.'

I would've just followed Bayat without asking for further explanation. I trusted him enough, believed he wanted to help us and would've told us what we needed to know, without instilling the fear Mayhaan did. He thundered up to us just as we were about to leave for the training.

'So, you're continuing with this madness?'

I didn't answer, not sure how to convince him we didn't have a choice.

'Has he told you yet what you're up against? The creatures?'

'Mayhaan,' Bayat interrupted, 'this isn't the time.'

'When will be the time? When the ferals are ripping out their throats?'

Fatima, who was leaning against Titus, gave a kind of strangled cry.

'Ferals?'

'Here.' Bayat handed me a long, wooden bow and a quiver of arrows, acting as if Mayhaan hadn't spoken. I wanted him to say something, to reassure us all and he saw it in my face. He gave a small shake of the head and I understood he needed me to stay silent, to let the fear that had taken hold at Mayhaan's words wash away, for the moment.

'Here.' I handed my bow and quiver to Emmaline as Bayat handed me another. I gave this to Matthew and then another to Titus. The second-last I kept for myself, slinging the bow awkwardly over my shoulder, as I'd seen Bayat do. I was only wearing my dress, having left Bayat's cloak in the cave. Although it was still cold, I suspected we'd be warmed up soon enough.

With the five of us thus armed, we left Mayhaan, Fatima and the caves. I turned to wave at my friend and saw Mayhaan talking intensely to her.

We walked down out of the mountains, going west, rather than retracing our steps. The decline was meandering, not steep and, with the air clear and the sun bright, I finally got to see the river, *our* river, from above: a thin, blue line weaving through the land. It looked magical, just as it did when you were next to it and I saw how it kept on going, off into the horizon, as if it never ended. In my heart, I followed the water to our village. How were they surviving? How exhausted was my mother and everyone else we had left behind? Had there been more deaths? I had to believe my father was still alive and what we were doing was the best way to help him.

When we got lower, and the river dropped out of sight, I remembered Omar and Zaana telling us to just keep on following it and wondered what they would say if they'd known about creatures called ferals who ripped out people's throats. I'm sure they would've never let us go.

On the north side of the mountains, away from the river, there was a huge rectangular field covered in thin yellow grass. Despite Mayhaan's haunting words, I was caught by the beauty of the place, bordered by the mountains on one side and the forest in the distance. I had never been anywhere so open. If it hadn't been for the others, I would've immediately started skipping and running, just like a young one again.

'This is where we start,' Bayat declared. He seemed to have stopped almost in the middle of the field and, like he'd read my mind, threw down his bag, bow and quiver, and began to run. 'Come on!'

I didn't need to be told twice. I threw off my own things and started sprinting after him. I almost expected him to cry 'can't catch me!' like Fatima and I had once done, but he just kept on running.

I glanced over my shoulder and saw the other three discarding their gear and starting to run, although none of them with my enthusiasm. Bayat and I were already at the other end of the field before they'd even made it halfway. When I expected him to pull up, to take a break, he veered to the left and continued on, hugging the edges of the space. I followed, jogging now like he was, realising this was not a fun gambol but the beginning of our training. I didn't look into the dark forest as we traversed its borders again and again and again. Nor did I gaze up at the vast mountains as they towered over my sweating, panting body. I kept my eyes on the muscles in Bayat's back.

My legs were screaming in pain before Bayat finally stopped running. He, too, was sweating, although he looked as if he could've kept on going. I threw myself onto the ground, as did Emmaline and Titus. Matthew, who was bright red and gasping for breath, didn't seem to even have the strength to sit down.

Caro arrived with water in gourds, hollowed out arlon-melons which, I'd learnt, were the main staple of the tribe. I drank from one and handed it on to Emmaline. None of us spoke, too exhausted to form words.

Whilst we sat and sipped, Bayat walked to the edge of the field, then plunged into the forest.

'Where's he gone?' I managed to whisper.

'To drown himself I hope,' Matthew said sourly. I wasn't completely surprised by the bitterness.

When he re-emerged, Bayat was carrying four long sacks, two on each shoulder. They seemed to be made from some coarse material, a bit like woven river reeds and, as he dumped one each in front of us, I saw, from the hole in the bottom seam, they were stuffed with the grass we were sitting on. They were about the length of a small child with a roundness at the end of them to represent a head.

'Over there.' Bayat pointed to the poles I had seen at the end of the field, the side closest to the mountains. Ten of them, hewn and polished from the many pine trees we had seen on our travels, and hammered into the ground in a row, about ten feet apart from one another.

I picked up and carried my sack to the pole at the far right, trying to manoeuvre it on with ease. Of course, the sack was much heavier when you had to lift it above your shoulders and, up close, the pole was taller than I'd imagined. Still, on the third try, I got it on.

Titus, Matthew and Emmaline had their sacks in place as well and we walked back to our bow and arrows. A line of us, each in front of our sack target.

We'd had the sense, at least, to spread out and I was grateful to have Matthew the furthest away from me. His seething irritation wasn't going to help my already jagged concentration. I looked closely at an arrow for the first time: its head was a finely sharpened triangle made of bone.

Bayat stood in front of us and effortlessly nocked the arrow into the furrowed rest, pointing it into the ground. Slowly he pulled back the string and in one swift, seamless movement, he lifted the bow, spun around and released. The missile flew through the air, a blur of deadly speed, and plunged right into the head of Matthew's sack.

I felt hopelessly weak. All morning I had tried to make the arrow fly and all morning, I had barely managed to keep the projectile inside the bow's stretch, let alone found the strength to pull the string far enough back to give it momentum. My hands were embedded with red lines and half-moons, the frustration of my fingernails digging in, and I was only just keeping tears at bay. To make things worse, Bayat seemed to be deliberately avoiding me.

Emmaline had grabbed his attention as soon

as we started, asking him to demonstrate again and then getting him to correct her position. I could see him occasionally glancing over to where I was, mainly hidden from his view by Titus. He didn't seem able to break away from Emmaline's determined attention.

'It's harder than it looks, hey?' Titus said to me at one point, about the only conversation we'd had since the running-away-from-the-cougar incident. How would he go when faced with these things called ferals? Would he run away again? How would I go? I watched as his arrow fell short of the sack although, at least, unlike my own weapon, it had actually left the bow.

'Do you need help?'

Bayat had materialised beside me. Concentrating on Titus, I hadn't noticed the break in Emmaline's monologue and was completely thrown by his appearance so close to me.

'Only if you can spare the time.' My resentment was impossible to conceal. I sounded petulant.

'She wanted help. She *asked* for help.'

I need help too! I wanted to shout, but I didn't.

'Do you want me to show you again?' He spoke quietly, gently. I nodded.

He moved even closer to me, standing to the right

so the bow was between us. I could smell him: the sweat from his running; the pine needles he'd been walking on; the grass sacks he'd been carrying. And underneath: him, his essence.

He put his hand over my left fingers and adjusted the way I was holding the bow, pushing my thumb down into a position instantly more comfortable. With his other hand he massaged my right fingers so they were no longer gripping the string and nock of the arrow, just holding them gently. The tension in my shoulder blades melted, though I still felt too tired to find the energy to fire. What I wanted, more than anything, was to put my forehead on his torso and for the rest of them to dissolve away. For it to be just us, in this field, lying in the grass.

His breathing was heavier and, as I turned my head to tell him this was too much, I was too pathetic to go on this journey, all I wanted to do was lie down in his arms, I realised his whole body was trembling.

'Don't look at me.' His voice was still strong. 'Look down the length of the shaft, to its point, to the bone.'

I did as he said, my vision tunnelling down to the tiny apex, to the very end of the arrow.

'Now,' he whispered in my ear, 'you must set her free.'

Without thinking, I straightened and let her fly.

The arrow spun straight and true, ploughing right into the heart of my sack body.

I knew the arrowhead had been made from the bone of my cougar as soon as it thumped into the pole. It was part of the connection I had felt with the animal in its death.

'That was incredible.'

Matthew, Emmaline and Titus were staring at me, their bows lowered. It was Titus who'd spoken. Bayat had moved away from my side and I felt strangely exposed, out there, in the field, having hit the target for the first time. My arm hung down and I couldn't imagine ever lifting it again, ever doing such a thing again. And aiming it at another living being? Impossible.

For the rest of the day, none of my arrows went as straight, but I did manage to fire again. And, more and more, they began to find their mark.

'It's time we headed back,' Bayat declared at last.

Wearily, we carried our sacks into the forest,

storing them in a small lean-to made of leaves and branches. We gathered up our empty bags, all our lunch of bread and fresh cougar eaten (though I was still avoiding the meat), and our bows and quivers.

We trudged back. Somehow the way seemed harder, less friendly and a few times I tripped, catching myself with my already aching hands. No one, not even Matthew, tried to help me. Fatigue had made everyone careless.

9

When Fatima limped up to us, eager to hear what we'd been doing for the day, to find out how our training had gone, I mumbled something about it being hard and tiring, and the look of us must have said enough, because she stopped asking questions, and started handing out our dinner, the same soup as the night before.

No one spoke, except to say 'thank you'. Soon it was only the six of us on the ridge, everyone else disappearing into their caves after finishing dinner. I suspected we were all too exhausted to move.

'Why exactly are we doing this?' Matthew asked, his voice full of weariness. 'Are you going to tell us about these ferals?'

Bayat yawned and so did I. I hoped he might suggest waiting until tomorrow.

'What did your parents tell you about the city they left?' he asked instead.

I thought of my father's whispered conversations and my mother's refusal to discuss the time before The Burning. I said nothing.

'Our parents left years before the fire-storm,' Emmaline was talking for Titus and her. 'My father and mother fled with his brother and his wife. They took a flock of goateeps, the goat-sheep blends they had developed, so they could have milk, wool, meat and skin, and they plunged into the last of the forests. They founded our village, ready for those who chose to escape Melney.'

I tried hard to keep my eyes open. I'd heard this genesis story before. All I wanted right now was to save that village. And I needed rest to do it.

Fatima cleared her throat.

'Mine came not long after. They wanted a different kind of life.'

'And your parents?' Bayat was looking at me.

I shrugged, still feeling sleepy.

'I don't know. They came with Matthew's parents, and were always grateful to Theodore and the rest for saving them. But they never told me the details.'

Matthew sighed.

'Neither did mine. My mother ghosted a few years

after my younger brother was born. My father never wanted to talk about the past.'

It'd been a long time since anyone had mentioned Matthew's mother, Petty. For the first six years of my life, she had been like a second mother. Even, though I would never say it out loud, like a *first* mother. It was Petty who gave me unconditional love. Zaana loved me, I knew that, but she always seemed to expect something more from me, as if I needed to fulfil an unspecified requirement, as if I had to make up for all that had gone wrong in the world. Petty wanted nothing from me, except my childish silliness and laughter.

'Ghosted?' Bayat asked.

'She disappeared, of her own free will.'

'Ah, we call it wandering. Going in search of something which can't be found.'

So the Mountain People had even less tolerance than the River People for those who believed in the possibility of more life out there.

'We are the same,' Bayat continued. 'Mayhaan and Bettina were our founders, they left before the End, what you call The Burning. They planted arlon-melon trees and developed hunting skills to make use of the rabrats, the rabbit-rats which had spread throughout this area, as well as sometimes hunting the cougar. We too have never gone back to Melney. Until, a year ago, we began to question why. We thought we might be able to scavenge some useful things there. That's when we discovered the city wasn't empty.'

'We?' I asked.

'My brother and I.'

'Your brother?'

'He's away. On his own hunting trip.'

I couldn't help staring at him. How could he have not mentioned a brother?

Matthew coughed.

'So you found these ferals?' he asked impatiently.

'*They* found us.'

We waited for him to go on. The fire crackled. I found myself looking into its red heart, the flames dancing.

'I can't even say what they are,' Bayat finally spoke again. 'When we first saw them, in the distance, we thought they were humans, maybe survivors who'd stayed in the city for some reason. But when they got closer, we saw there was something .... else ... in them. Something ... wild.'

'And they are dangerous?' Titus asked.

I could feel our fear.

'They can be killed. My brother and I ... survived.'

There was something in his pause which, if we'd been alone, I would have pursued. As it was, I decided we had to push this fear away and remember what our journey was about.

'The drug is there, Bayat. That will save our people.' Emmaline, Titus, Fatima and Matthew were nodding. 'We just have to risk it.'

Out of the darkness, a figure appeared. Mayhaan stepped into the weak glow of the firelight. I hadn't heard him approach, but I guess he had been a hunter too.

'I would risk no one,' he said, showing he had been listening in to the conversation. 'Especially not for a lost cause.'

'You will risk me.' Bayat, like I had, looked into the flames of the fire, solemn and, it seemed, unafraid. 'I will be going with them, Mayhaan. I will return to the city and I will help them fight the ferals to find this cure.'

My heart did a leap and I smiled. He would be coming with us! He would protect us from these creatures and guide us through Melney. Everything would be okay, everything would be easy.

He seemed to read my optimistic mind.

'I'm just one person, Pandora,' he said. 'It'll take more than that for us to be safe. My brother and

I ... survived ... because we have been hunters all our lives. A few days training cannot give you those skills. But I will do my best.'

Mayhaan's face danced with shadows. I could see the sadness in it.

'If that is what you wish, Bayat.'

We rose to go to our caves, all of us moving slowly and wearily. Only as we started the walk back to our sleeping quarters did I realise Bayat hadn't told us the story of *his* parents' leaving the city, nor where they were now.

That night, despite going to bed with my head swirling with thoughts, I slept heavily and woke the next morning feeling as if no time had passed, as if I could close my eyes again and sleep for a season. I forced myself to rise, trying to stifle the groans as every muscle protested, from my neck to the soles of my feet.

Emmaline had already gone out for breakfast. Fatima was sitting on one of the rocks, her sore leg sticking out awkwardly, as she still couldn't cross her ankle over the other. With all the horrid visions created the night before, I longed to get out into the daylight.

'Pan?' Fatima obviously had other ideas. 'I need to talk to you.'

I tried not to sigh. I didn't have the energy for a heart-to-heart with Fatima but the more days went by, the more I realised my needs were rarely what counted. Fatima's bruise and cut were healing well but her face was still marked with worry.

'What's the matter, Fat?'

'What am I going to do?'

I didn't know what she was referring to: was this about Titus, her sprained ankle, today's training or the journey to the city?

'You just need to rest.'

I shouldn't have but I felt envious of her. How much better life would be if I didn't have to go to the field today, if I didn't have to sweat and fail in front of Bayat, if I could just stay here in the cave and sleep ...?

'What good am I going to be?' Fatima continued. 'Even if my ankle has healed by the time you leave, I won't be any use. I'm too scared, Pan. I'm not like you, I can't be brave.'

Brave? Never had I thought of myself as brave. I couldn't think it was bravery which made me save Fatima from the cougar. I'd just done what had to be done.

'I was going to go with him, you know,' Fatima was looking down at her hands.

I frowned, again I didn't know what she was talking about.

'With Titus. I was going to run from the cougar, just like he did. Abandon you. I just didn't have the time. And I will do it again. I can't face these creatures they are talking about. Mayhaan told me Bayat and his brother only just escaped. All night I had nightmares.'

What could I tell her? I thought she was wrong? I believed she'd find some inner strength to face the demons? I didn't believe it of myself, let alone her. I was sure I didn't have nightmares only because I was so tired.

'I only came because I thought it would be what my parents would want. For me to stay with Titus, my Chosen.'

'You could ... go home?'

She looked as if I'd slapped her. Too late, I knew I'd said the wrong thing. She had wanted me to reassure her, to pretend I knew everything was going to be fine, that she was going to be strong enough.

'I knew you didn't believe in me either.'

'No, I ...'

'Don't worry, Pan.' Pushing herself up from the

rock, she gingerly limped to the cave's entrance. 'I'll try not to be too much of a burden to you.'

She stormed out, as dramatically as she'd always done, except this time she had the limp to make it look even less convincing.

In the field the sun shone bright, as if to mock the darkness of our moods. This time, we were throwing knives at the sacks, taking turns – one, two, three and four – to aim for the centre of the target, the heart, before retrieving our weapon and trying again. Bayat walked behind us, making suggestions for how to improve our aim or increase our distance. He had barely said good morning to me.

Only once did I manage to get the short-handled blade near the sack into what would have been a right thigh. The rest of my throws were either too short or off-target. I couldn't stop thinking of the sacks of grass as people. Even if they were 'wild' people, I still hated the thought of sharp metal lodging into bloody flesh.

'You're not trying hard enough.' Bayat was standing next to me again. This time, there was nothing gentle in his demeanour.

'I'm trying my best.'

'No, you're not.'

What more did he want from me? I put my feet into the stance he had shown us. For a moment, I hoped he might come close again and help me hold the knife. Instead, he actually stepped away, crossing his arms and watching me critically.

'Is that how I showed you to hold it?'

I looked down and tried to remember what he'd said about the grip. Was it thumb up or around? I'd been swapping between the two because I didn't want to ask.

'And why is your left foot forward? You use your strongest leg to give you support.'

I changed my legs around and heard the thwack of Titus's knife hitting the pole. It was my turn, the others were waiting.

'Why are you looking at the knife? Concentrate on the target.'

He had not talked to me like this before. I swallowed, trying to get rid of the rising lump in my throat. His face looked like I remembered it from the moment at the river: hard and unforgiving.

'Why are you waiting? Will the feral wait until you're good and ready? You have to get them in their heart.'

My hand was sweaty and I could barely see the target for the tears in my eyes. I threw anyway, thrusting out my arm with all the strength I had left. It thudded uselessly into the grass, four feet short of the pretend enemy.

'So, I guess you'd be dead.'

I couldn't take this any longer. I did what I had vowed, after Titus, I wouldn't do: I ran away.

I could hear Matthew shouting behind me, 'Pan! Pan!' – it was always Matthew calling out for me – and I could have sworn I heard Emmaline laughing. I should've taken the path back to the caves, at least there I might have found food and water to comfort me. Then I remembered Fatima and how she hated me as well so I kept going into the forest, following the track we'd gone down to the shelter for the sacks and kept going, losing myself in the twists and turns, until I was far enough away from humiliation, and him.

I stopped, breathing in the quiet.

Why had he done that to me? Yesterday, he'd helped me shoot so perfectly. I'd felt close to him. Today, he'd made me look like a fool. I felt as far from him as the stars in the sky.

I lay down on the forest floor and, finally, let my tears run free. Such a relief to have them falling down my face, dropping to the ground, watering the trees. I wanted my father's arms around me, as they had always been before, and my mother's quiet concern: 'what's happened, my love?' I wanted to be waking up to the crack in the ceiling and the sound of the goateeps bleating and the promise of a safe and ordinary day. I wanted Fatima's laughter and Matthew's classroom questions. I wanted the past, a place I knew I couldn't get back to.

I heard feet crunching on the pine needles and sat up. I'd stopped crying. I fully expected Matthew to appear and, at the very least, offer a sympathetic hug. But it was Bayat. He had his cloak in his arms – I'd worn it this morning for the walk to the field – and, without saying a word, squatted next to me and placed it around my shoulders. He sat beside me. Neither of us looked at one another.

'Matthew wanted to come to you instead.'

'How did you convince him not to?'

He shrugged.

'I can be quite ... authoritative when I need to be.'

I laughed. 'Yeah, I noticed.'

In the silence, I might have expected an apology.

He picked up a pine needle and bent it in two.

'I don't like this forest much, these ... leaves ... kill everything beneath them. Nothing grows or lives in here. Listen.'

He was right. There were no sounds, no rabrats crawling or owls calling. It should have been creepy, though with Bayat beside me, everything felt ... not exactly safe, only less scary.

'This isn't a game, Pandora. Someone ... you ... could get killed.'

'I know.'

'Do you?'

I watched as he rubbed the broken needle between his thumb and his finger. I wanted him to, at least, acknowledge what he thought of me.

'You don't think I can do this, do you? You think I'm weak. Unlike Emmaline.'

He looked up and frowned at me.

'Emmaline?'

Then he smiled. He threw the needle onto the ground and put his hand into the pocket of his pants. He showed me his fist, then turned it over and opened his fingers. On his palm sat a stone.

'Do you remember this?'

The river stone was a deep green with a hairline crack down its centre. The one I threw to scare away the cougar, the first time we saw one another. He had kept it. He carried it with him.

I nodded. I couldn't even imagine saying anything.

'You're not weak, Pandora. From the first moment I saw you, I ...'

I blushed, remembering exactly how much of me he'd seen in the river. My nakedness.

'Sorry, I didn't mean ...'

He was stumbling again and I wanted to help him. I closed my hand around the hand which held the stone and reached up to put my lips to his. I had never kissed anyone like this before and didn't quite know what to do but his other hand found its way to the back of my neck and he gently pushed me into him, so our mouths were opening and I felt the hot rush through my body and wanted only to be closer to him.

If this was what it felt like to be in love, I never wanted anything else. Every part of me was on fire and even as it seemed like I couldn't breathe, I was more alive than I'd ever been.

His hand ran down my bare arm, his cloak had slipped off my shoulders, and I felt the heat of his palm against my skin. It moved up my thigh and stopped. We pulled away from each other at the same moment. Panting, like we had just run the lengths of the field. A kind of confusion. Had I really wanted him to stop? I knew where this could go. Was I really ready for it? Could I do this to my parents? To Matthew?

'Pan! Pan?'

As if I'd conjured him up with my thoughts, Matthew's shouts echoed into the forest. I couldn't see him yet, so he couldn't see us. I pulled the cloak back around me and stood. Bayat did the same. I tried to slow down my breathing, to make myself seem … normal. Like nothing had happened. Was that even possible? I couldn't imagine Matthew not being able to see how much things had changed, in just one moment.

'Pan? Are you all right?'

Matthew strode down the track, his face full of worry. He held his hat in his hand and his white skin glistened with sweat. I figured Bayat had got them to do some physical task before coming after me. Matthew had obviously had enough of it.

I wanted to be irritated with him for constantly following me. At the same time, I knew it came from his own version of care. Maybe he'd saved me from doing something with Bayat I would regret? Or had we saved ourselves?

'I'm fine, Matthew,' I said. 'Thanks for coming to check on me.'

He looked surprised. This was the most I'd spoken to him since our conversation amongst the boulders. In the corner of my eye, I saw Bayat looking sullen.

'Shouldn't we be getting on?' Matthew's dislike of Bayat was no longer under the surface. He could barely be polite to him.

Bayat pushed past him, heading back towards our training ground.

Matthew stood in front of me and pushed a strand of hair over my ear.

'Don't let him bully you.'

The residue of Bayat's touch was still on my skin and I couldn't believe Matthew could be so blind to my feelings.

'I'm going to protect you, Pan.'

One sign of kindness and he had reclaimed me as his own! Unbelievable! I swatted his hand away.

'All of us are going to have a hard enough time looking after ourselves. The only person who's going to protect me is *me*, Matthew.'

In the distance, I heard the 'thwack, thwack, thwack' of knives hitting wood once again.

The next day Bayat announced we would try hand-to-hand fighting.

'I hope they won't get this close but ... we need to be prepared in case they do.'

He had not spoken directly to me the whole of the night before, retreating to his cave as soon as dinner was eaten. I didn't know where his home was, in the warren of the tribe's hollowed-out dwellings, so I couldn't have gone after him, even if I had wanted to.

'Pandora, you'll start with Emmaline. Matthew, you're with Titus.'

While I knew it was a good idea to begin going up against someone of your own strength, I couldn't help wonder if this pairing was a deliberate attempt to keep me away from Matthew. I hadn't had a chance to talk to Bayat about the ways of our village, about being Chosen. Or, maybe, if I was honest, I hadn't given myself the chance. What would happen if I spoke the truth? If he understood what was supposed to happen between Matthew and I? How traitorous it was that I'd kissed him?

Emmaline stood opposite me. She had finally cut her dress just below the knee, conceding its former length was a hazard in our training. Neither of us moved.

'Emmaline,' Bayat said, 'what would be your first line of attack?'

I thought back to summer days in the time before our Blossoming when we had mock wars with one another: Fatima, Matthew, Cassie and I versus Emmaline and Titus. We marked out large circles of territory using sticks in the dirt, setting up worlds with mats and collections of stones. Then we'd throw the pebbles at one another, trying to invade each other's land. We didn't really want to go to the other side, it was just a way to tease, to irritate one another. They were small stones, which couldn't do much harm. One time Emmaline and Titus, though, tried to kidnap Fatima, carrying her by her arms and legs as a joke, calling out to us that we'd have to pay a ransom. Fatima had screamed so loudly the adults had come running, thinking her terror was real. They were thunderously angry and it put an end to those games.

'Pandora? Are you ready?'

I came back to the present.

Emmaline twisted her whole body to the side and tried to land her right leg into my stomach. Instinctively, I jumped back and grabbed her by the ankle. She twisted it out of my hands, putting me off balance. I fell to the side and she was on top of me, pushing me into the ground, pinning my arms into the grass. She had left enough space so I could bunch up my legs and push both my feet into her torso, sending her sprawling away. She recovered quickly and ran at me again. I rolled to the side, pushing myself back up to stand. We stared at one another, drawing deep breaths. I was amazed at how agile she was and how willing to attack me. Even though this was just practice, her heart was definitely in it.

It was my turn. Like her, I raised my leg to kick but, unlike her, I aimed for her kneecap. She cried out in pain as I hit bone and she fell onto her backside. I stepped back, expecting her to get up again. Later, I remembered the pause, the tiny moment between my hit and her reaction.

'Oh, it hurts!' she suddenly cried out, lying on her side, gripping her knee with both hands.

My small tingle of triumph evaporated.

'Emmaline? I'm so sorry.'

Bayat and Titus both knelt down beside her. Fatima, who had come to watch for the first time, stood with Matthew. Once again, I seemed to be alone, separated from them all.

'It really hurts!' Emmaline repeated. I felt sure this was not real, whatever pain she had wasn't equal to the fuss she was making.

'I'll have to take her back.' Bayat helped her to stand, his arm around her waist. Emmaline was keeping her head down and began to hop along beside him.

They made their way along the track, towards the caves.

Bayat didn't return for the rest of the morning. I spent the time showing Fatima how to shoot. My own efforts were getting better and better even when I didn't have Bayat whispering in my ear, although my concentration wasn't the best as I spent every second moment glancing over to the pathway, hoping to see him come back. Fatima still wasn't really talking to me, her face unsmiling as I guided her through the motions.

Matthew and Titus did some mock fighting. They decided to use the blunt-ended poles Bayat had brought along, blocking and sparring with one another in a way that seemed safer than flesh on flesh. It looked more like a dance.

Fatima wanted to rest her leg after a short amount of time, so we sat and watched. I was astounded by how muscular and strong the boys were. Titus moved with such assurance, his expression of determination nothing like the night of the cougar.

And Matthew, whose words had irritated me only yesterday, darted across the field, attacking, then wisely retreating, then pushing forward again.

'I'm sorry I said the wrong thing, Fat,' I tried.

'I know you think I am pathetic, dedicating myself to Titus like an idiot.'

'That's not true. I wish I could ...'

'What? Do the same with Matthew?'

I should've guessed Fatima would be able to tell what was going on in my head, and heart. She could see I didn't have the same loyalty to our parent's wishes.

'Matthew is the best person we know,' Fatima's eyes were following the two boys as they danced across the grass.

'Yes.'

'So I hope you will do what is right, Pan,' Fatima spoke with that quiet determination I'd seen in her on the day of the Blossoming. 'We have a responsibility. To our people. To the land.'

I nodded, unable to say anything.

Matthew and Titus's bare torsos shone in the mountain sun. They were truly beautiful. Despite what Bayat thought, I saw we were not as unprepared as he'd presumed. It wasn't just his few days of training that would save us. We may not have been hunters, but we had survived since The Burning. We were capable, I believed, of anything.

Emmaline sat in our cave, her back against the wall, with her leg raised slightly above the ground, resting on a rock. Wrapped around her, I saw with a flip of my stomach, was Bayat's cloak, the one he had supposedly given to me. I'd left it behind this morning and now it looked like it had been transferred to Emmaline.

'How's your knee?' I asked.

'It's fine,' Emmaline breezily replied. 'It will be all better by tomorrow.'

'Really?'

'Of course.' She had a smirk on her face which she forced into a little, sly smile. 'Aren't you going to ask me how we spent the morning?'

The word 'we' was enough to clench my teeth. I decided it was time to go and have my lunch.

'Do you need anything, Emmaline?' My politeness gave her nowhere to go, no more digs to make.

'No … thanks.'

As I left, I tried not to imagine Bayat and her sitting here together, laughing or talking or … worse.

I reminded myself he had kept the river stone and how he had smiled when I revealed my jealousy of Emmaline. But maybe that smile had meant something else? I wanted to trust him, only I found I didn't trust Emmaline. After all, I'd just decided the River People were capable of anything.

10

By the end of the fourth day, I began to think my kiss with Bayat had been a dream.

He pushed us hard, quietly and forcefully ordering us about. I could've sworn he was the hardest with me, picking on the way I tried to wrestle Matthew to the ground, or the strength of my knife throws, even when they actually landed in the, by now, sagging grass sacks, or the amount of laps of the field I was able to do without stopping, despite the fact I was only second to Titus. He did, at least, recognise my shooting skills and had me practise with the bow and arrow the most. I was the best of us though still not, obviously, as good as him.

I tried to hold onto the belief Bayat was pushing me this way to help me prepare more, to help me survive. I just wondered why he couldn't use an occasional word of praise or encouragement.

Thankfully, I didn't see any connection between him and the miraculously recovered Emmaline, although I was probably sweating and panting too much to notice any special looks.

I just couldn't wait for the sun to start setting, to trudge back to the caves and lie my aching body down. Bayat had told us the next day would be a rest day before we resumed our journey. Again, no one protested, no one argued for us to begin earlier, to set off as soon as we could. It was as if we'd pushed the scenes of our sick village to the very back of our minds, hidden them away like river stones, kept in our pockets, only to be brought out when we were ready for them.

That night I finally ate cougar meat. Caro came to sit beside me around the central fire pit where we had all our dinners and quietly handed me a small piece of what looked like the dried goateep we had brought with us from home. I knew there were no goateeps – the milk-like substance came from the pulverised argon-melon they grew on the eastern side of the mountains – and this must be something they'd hunted.

'It's not *your* cougar. It's from an older hunt,' he whispered. 'Bayat told me to tell you that.'

I couldn't see Bayat in the circle around the fire. Why hadn't he brought it to me himself?

'He also told me not to tell you that he told me to tell you.'

Caro had a cheeky grin on his face.

'But I guess I stuffed that up.'

He giggled.

I took a tiny bite of the chewy substance. It was stronger tasting than goateep. I swallowed it, knowing I had to get rid of any sense of betrayal. In my mind I saw the shiny pupils of the great cat, just before she was about to pounce, but I pushed the image away.

'Caro, what's a reader?'

It looked like I wasn't going to get a chance to ask Bayat.

Caro stopped smiling. He looked around, as if to make sure no one was listening.

'My father believes that humans are changing. That, since the world passed through its End, there are those who have access to another layer of reality.'

'Visions?'

'Yes.'

'Of the past or the present or ... the future?'

'I don't know. You're the first person I've ever seen have one.'

I closed my eyes, trying to remember that time after the cougar attack. I opened them again.

'Do all the Mountain People believe this?'

Caro shook his head. 'My mother says it isn't logical.'

'Where did the idea of a reader come from?'

Caro grinned his grin again.

'Bayat, of course. He's had visions but I've never been there during one. My father says this is why he is such a great hunter. I wish I was a reader.'

'Bayat sees the cougar?'

'I guess so.'

I took another bite of the meat, chewing slowly.

That night I slept like a dead person and woke with a deep sense of foreboding. This was supposed to be our day of rest. Still, I got up and snuck out of the cave. The sun was just rising as a thin orange line on the horizon and the tribe was beginning to wake. I could hear vague clattering inside the caves and saw a few familiar figures emerging. The air smelt of last night's fire, the mountain mist clung to my cheeks and I pulled my cloak, which Emmaline had wordlessly left in my sleeping space a few days before, into my body, trying to eliminate the gaps where the freezing wind nipped in.

On the large stone ridge, I saw an even more familiar shape. Bayat stood, his back to me. He seemed to be looking up, gazing at the higher cave openings.

I walked up the path towards Bayat and he turned, hearing me approach. His arms were crossed, his face set harder than I had ever seen. The corners of his mouth had thin lines coming off them, so entrenched it seemed impossible I had not noticed them before. I slowed my steps. The nearer I drew to him, the more fearful I became. Was this what I had been dreading since waking? Had Bayat really become a stranger to me?

Only as I got close enough to see his eyes did I understand. They were not brown, not the same river mud colour as my own. Blue, flecked with green. The eyes of a stranger. Bayat's brother. I had not expected him to be so similar and realised he was more than just a brother: they were twins.

'Who are you?' His voice was also like Bayat's, except I had never heard him speak this rudely.

'She is our guest.' Here was Bayat, quickly striding

up behind his brother. His hair was tousled, as if he'd just woken up.

'Since when do we have Babblers as our guests?'

When Caro had called us Babblers, it had an element of sweetness to it. Bayat's brother made it sound contemptuous. I couldn't imagine what my people might have done to deserve this lack of respect, or why Bayat's brother would want to look at me with such disdain.

'I'll explain it all to you, Oyan. Come and eat first.'

Bayat was trying to distract his brother, to break the scornful look Oyan had fixed on me.

'You didn't answer my question, river girl,' Oyan said, taking steps towards me.

I was tempted to tell him to go drown himself and only stopped myself when I saw Bayat's distressed face.

'My name is ... Pan.' Already I knew I didn't want Oyan using my full name, the way Bayat did. Under his eyes I saw the faintest remnant of black ochre and remembered why he'd been away. 'Did you have a good hunt?'

Oyan's lips drew even thinner. Over his brother's shoulder, Bayat shook his head, trying to warn me away from this subject, too late.

'Not all of us are as ... lucky as my brother.'

'Or gifted, maybe? Or skilled?'

Oyan grinned grotesquely. He was only an arm's length away from me and I could barely believe these two boys could have shared the same mother.

'Gifted? Ha! Did you hear that, Bayat? You've got an admirer.'

I could feel myself blushing and, to my horror, noticed Bayat going red too. He was supposed to be the cool one, capable of making me doubt his feelings completely. Now he was making it all too easy for Oyan to mock us.

Oyan had turned to check on the effect of his teasing and saw its success.

'Oh, but it looks like I didn't need to tell you.'

He swung back and appraised me anew, running his eyes up and down my body, as if I was some kind of animal whose quality needed to be tested.

'Was she the best of them?'

I left a pause, long enough for Bayat to smack him in the face, which he didn't do, and walked away. I heard raised voices behind me. The seething buzz in my ears blocked out the words and all I could think was how I wanted to get as far away as possible from this hideous creature, posing as the close kin of the one I loved, without any similarity except the same beautiful frame.

I lay on my back in the sun, a large patch of moss beneath me. I'd left the tribe behind, travelling down the mountain in the same direction we had arrived and crossing the river. Although I was so far from home, it felt good to be on this side, on *my* people's side, as if the ground could connect me back to the village. What were they doing now? Who was on nursing duty? Had anyone else ... died? My stomach twisted in dread again.

Above me the sky was clear and blue and without the mist of the highlands, the air was not chilled, just cool and fresh. I had to keep breathing deeply. Relax. If I let myself think of home my heart beat too fast, the panic of imagining the worst. I had to push it away.

I focused on the throbbing of my brand. Since we'd begun training I'd been trying to ignore my shoulder and the way in which the muscles there had begun to ache. Now I could allow the pain to enter me. Every time I inhaled I felt the three vertical lines, every time I exhaled I felt the gashes from the cat's claws.

I closed my eyes and stretched my arms above my head, trying to ease the throb.

'I brought you a salve.'

I opened my eyes to find him standing above me, a shadow blocking out the light. For a tiny moment, I was scared it might be Oyan, he might have followed me to continue his humiliation. The eyes looking down at me, though, were the same ones I had locked onto that day at the river. It seemed a long time ago, even though I knew it was less than one cycle of the moon.

Bayat held a small wooden bowl. I sat up and he knelt down to show me a thick, white paste inside it.

'Bettina says it works well to help muscle pain.'

'How did you know?'

'It wasn't hard to notice you wince every time you threw a knife or shot an arrow.'

And here I was thinking I'd hidden it so well.

'Do you want me to ...?'

I turned my back on him.

'So this is your ... mark?' His fingers traced the scarred flesh. I tried to sit still, to not let myself feel anything too much.

'Yes, the brand of the River People.'

'They *brand* you. Like they used to do with animals.'

'It's part of a ... ritual.'

'The cat's scratches have cut into it. It's almost as if she's ... traced the lines.'

'That's not possible.'

'It's what it looks like.'

He applied the cream of the healing lotion, his fingertips running over the wavy lines and the circle, slowly and carefully. Even as his hands were cold, I could feel the heat in the rest of me, the pounding of my heart in my ears. I could barely think of what he'd just told me about the scratches. Now I could only concentrate on the thrill of his touch, how I never wanted this to end, how I wanted this to go on, and further. How I couldn't let that happen. How was I going to stop this? It was impossible to allow him to be so close and impossible to not let him be so close.

'What else do you do in this ... ritual?' His voice was quiet, but there was also tension in it, as if he too was forcing himself to hold back.

I closed my eyes again, lowering my head. This was the moment to talk about Matthew, to explain all he was supposed to be to me, to make it clear why we couldn't do what I so desperately wanted to do. I thought again of our kiss in the forest, of where it might have continued if not for Matthew's interruption.

'We get a new dress,' I said, taking the coward's way out.

His fingers paused. I couldn't tell if it was the salve or his touch which was making me feel better. The pain seemed to have disappeared.

If I spoke the words, if I told him what I knew he already suspected – I was supposed to be with Matthew – I feared everything would end between us, even before it had really begun. He would switch to Emmaline, who had no ties, nothing to stop her. I couldn't actually understand why he had shown this amount of interest in me in the first place and if I couldn't understand it, why should he? Maybe it was a huge mistake. A mistake which would be fixed when he left me and chose Emmaline.

What was the point in fighting the inevitable? I couldn't change myself into someone who could recite poetry flawlessly or move gracefully like a fish through water. I felt angry, though I didn't exactly know who at.

I stood. I moved away from where Bayat remained seated, stepping off the mossy ground and onto the pebbles of the riverbank. For a moment, I concentrated on the water, looking at the range of colours in the rocks, the greens and the greys, the flash of purple, the deep brown. I wondered if Bayat always carried 'our' stone, or if he had just happened to have it that day. I suddenly felt suspicious of everything. Maybe this was about something else, some Mountain People trick, to make me look like an idiot? In my heart, I knew this came from Oyan's taunting. *Was she the best of them?*

'Why do you like me?'

Bayat was smiling.

'Now, there's a way to change a conversation.'

I knew he wanted to make everything light. I couldn't stop myself going into the dark, to the worst parts of myself.

'I'm not beautiful, I know that. I'm not much of a runner, or a fighter. I made Fatima mad at me and she's supposed to be my best friend. Why do you like me? Is it only because I'm a reader like you? That doesn't make me special. I think I only volunteered to go to the city because I wanted to get away from what the village expects of me. I love my parents but I've never been good enough for my mother. And now they will die because we don't have a chance against the ferals.'

I didn't seem able to stop myself.

'What if my parents are dead? What if it's all over already?'

'Hey! Hey ...'

Bayat jumped up and strode toward me. I couldn't breathe properly, gulping in air as if I'd just sprinted around the training field.

'Stop this.'

I wanted to breathe normally. I couldn't get it out of my head: *was she the best of them?* Bayat tried to put his hands on my shoulders. I ducked back, shrugging him away. My feet were in the river water, the coolness startling me a little. Still, I kept panting.

'What if I've already failed them?'

'Pandora, I can't tell you what is going on in your village. We can only hope ... And I can't tell you exactly why I like you. I don't have the words. I don't know ...'

This was not what I needed. I needed him to find the words, even if they were made up, even if they were untrue. Just like Fatima had needed me to make up false assurances. I waited, hoping something would shift, somehow he would say what I wanted.

Then, in the distance, we heard a roar. It was the same sound I had heard coming from Bayat's mouth when he announced our arrival to the tribe. Only this cry, I couldn't think of any other way to describe it, was filled with danger, not joy.

'It's Oyan,' Bayat said, his face turning pale.

'Something terrible has happened.'

Whatever state I had just been in, whatever palpitations I'd just been experiencing, disappeared in an instant. We both splashed through the river and ran back towards the mountains.

At the very least, the training had ensured I could just keep up with Bayat and as we sped along the path to the caves, I realised my muscles were stronger than they'd ever been. I'd started to learn how quickly the brain could jump from one state to another, how it seemed to have hole after hole, like caves, where it kept all these bubbling thoughts which, only a moment before, felt like the only thing you could ever think about. By the time we'd got to the stone ridge, where I could see Emmaline, Titus, Fatima, Matthew, Caro and Oyan gathered, along with many of the tribe who I didn't know by name, the panic about what might have happened had cleared my head of my fears about my parents and Bayat. My panting was due to exertion, not imagination.

Oyan stormed up to Bayat, hardly waiting for him to catch his breath.

'They've brought the disease.'

Caro ran up and threw his arms around me, burrowing his head into my stomach. He was a little boy again.

'It's my mother,' he whispered.

Bettina. I pictured her round, gentle face. She had fed me and even, I realised, healed me without attracting attention, without seeming to want gratitude. A memory of her hands cupping bowls and handing them out.

I knew now why Mayhaan was nowhere to be seen.

'And there are others,' Oyan spat. If he had disliked me before, now he seemed to be looking at me with undisguised hatred. I lay my hand on the back of Caro's head, trying to soothe him.

'How many?' Bayat asked. He did not appear to be asking about anyone in particular, another confirmation of his solitary status, if you didn't count Oyan and, for the moment, I certainly didn't want to.

'I … I don't know.' This request for specific information threw Oyan off guard. He seemed to have been too busy gloating.

'Then, perhaps,' Bayat said forcefully, 'we should start by checking all the caves, find out who needs help nursing their sick and get the River People to tell us the best way to treat them.'

At last, Oyan looked shame-faced. It lasted for a short moment, before he started bellowing orders. Those who were gathered broke apart, scattering in all directions, hurrying off to make themselves useful or to return to their bedridden loved ones. I saw Emmaline and Fatima consulting with a group of women about vessels to boil water, and Titus and Matthew headed off with some men to collect more fire wood. Bayat had given me just a fleeting look before disappearing up one of the paths, presumably to take his inventory. I wondered how many would be taken ill. It was my village repeated. There was no reason to believe the numbers would be any better.

Amongst all the busyness, I continued to stroke Caro's hair, unwilling to do what I knew I had to. If I was learning about how my brain could shift, I was also learning about how my fear could change so quickly from one moment to the next.

Yes, I was afraid of death, of how many of the tribe might be lost. But this was something I could face, I had done it before. No, I was more afraid of the tangible result of this new disaster. I was more afraid of Mayhaan's anger.

I guess you can never really know how people are going to react to a threat. I had expected Mayhaan to rant and rail against me, to be sickened by the sight of me. Instead, when I walked into the smoky cave holding Caro's hand, Mayhaan simply raised his head from his place sitting beside the prostrate Bettina, gripping her hand, and gave me a small nod, as if to say I had a right to be there.

Bettina looked to be in the same state as my father. She was pale and her breathing was laboured. She didn't have the rose-coloured patches we'd observed on the three corpses so I thought there was hope and told Mayhaan and Caro this. I explained everything my mother had advised us to do during the initial outbreak, reassuring Mayhaan this was already taking place in the tribe, under Bayat's direction. At one point, I could tell Mayhaan was conflicted between his duty to be a leader and his desire to stay by Bettina's side. He didn't seem able to let go of her hand and, with Caro on her other side, she was well-watched over.

I sat for a moment, not knowing where to look. On the walls I saw there were deep furrows – like the marks on our Growing Tree, I realised these must be Caro's life line – as well as pictures painted in black ochre: a bird in flight, maybe an eagle, and two stick-figures, waving hello (or farewell) surrounded by swirls of black which might have been flames. I wanted to ask who had done them, but knew this wasn't the time. I went to leave.

'Pan,' Mayhaan called from his nursing position. I paused, waiting for the tirade of blame and guilt to come at last. 'You will bring back enough medicine, won't you? For us all?'

This blessing filled me with the most determination I had felt since leaving the village.

'I promise.'

The rest of the day and half the night were like a return to a nightmare. Carrying and nursing the sick, building fires, cleaning up vomit and faeces. In many ways, it was worse than the village, because the ill couldn't be gathered into one central place, the stone ridge was too open air, so we had to go from cave to cave, doing rounds until it seemed like all we'd ever done was rotate from one overheated, stench-filled chamber to the next, losing track of who was who, of which patient was showing signs of revival, of which family was suffering the most.

Bayat reported at mid-morning there were no

dead yet. For a while, I optimistically thought maybe the Mountain People had better resistance than us but two older members of the tribe had died by the end of the day.

I couldn't watch as Bayat and the others carried the bodies down into the forest where we had dug out graves. Like us, the tribe didn't have a dedicated burial site. Until this time we'd only had single deaths to contend with. Besides, in my village, each family would deliver their dead back into the river while the Mountain People, I learned, usually burnt their lost. Everyone had agreed this was too risky – we had no idea if burning the bodies might spread the disease – so a place had been found to deposit them into the soil.

I was distracted and fatigued enough not to be able to think often of my guilt but it was always there, nagging at the back of my mind. Had we brought this to these people? I knew Oyan thought so. Mayhaan's mildness had made me think he might not be so sure. Perhaps this sickness was going to come to them anyway? Perhaps it was only a coincidence we happened to be here? After all, we had been with them for four days without any sign of it. Could it really hide itself in us and magically appear when it wanted? I didn't know enough about how such things worked and wished I could talk to my mother. I felt sure she would be able to explain it by now, to have made sense of what was happening, of how we could continue to be so close to the sickness, and not have any of the signs of it ourselves. I had insisted to Mayhaan we weren't carriers. How did I really know?

I wished I had time to talk to Bayat about it. This was impossible. He had become the tribe's leader in Mayhaan's absence, along with Oyan, although I noticed how more of the tribe members went to Bayat first, only resorting to his brother when he wasn't available.

As night fell, the moans and cries of the sick quietened, most of them falling into restless sleep. I knew so many of the tribe would be up during the dark hours, tending to their needs, cleaning the sweat off their foreheads. Every one of the ill reminded me of my father. He was always with me now, his drained face whispering his goodbye before my departure.

'Stay safe,' he'd said. 'You are everything to us.'

I hadn't wanted to think about those words. Hadn't wanted to own them, to have the burden of them. I didn't want to be everything to anyone. I loved my parents, but my life was my own, wasn't it?

I couldn't keep myself alive just for their sake, could I? It had to be for more than that.

Bayat found us – Emmaline, Fatima and I were washing out cups at one of the stone troughs – and told us to go to bed.

'We'll leave for the city as soon as the sun rises,' he said.

This is my fifth and final night with the tribe. I sit, wrapped in Bayat's cloak, and know I should be sleeping but am listening instead to the screech owls. When Caro told me this was their name he had his cheekiest grin on. I hate to compare it to the way I saw him last, his face without any light, without any sign of ever having laughed.

Bayat hadn't really looked at me as he said goodnight to the three of us and I wonder if he has the same opinion as Oyan: we've brought this sickness to them, these deaths are our fault. Or, if you want to look at it more closely, *my* fault. Because I'm the one who insisted we travel to the city, I'm the one who pushed us here. Did I really believe I could save everyone or was it just the prospect of leaving the village like I'd confessed to Bayat?

I remember one of our classes where Rama talked to us about motivation.

'If you are doing something which you believe to be good, but which results in something bad, are you a good or a bad person?'

'No one is simply good or bad,' Matthew had replied, always understanding so much more quickly than the rest of us. 'Actions are a result of decisions made consciously and unconsciously. They might have consequences you never dreamed of, never imagined.'

'But there are evil people,' Fatima had chimed in. 'We know that. They brought about The Burning.'

'No one can say they are pure anything, that they are just one thing,' Matthew insisted. 'We're all a mix.'

Rama paused. 'A man called Edmund Burke once said, "The only thing necessary for the triumph of evil is for good men to do nothing."'

'So did our parents do nothing to stop The Burning?' I asked, and the class fell silent.

We are not special. We are just survivors.

This is what I have been taught all my life. But if

we are just survivors, if we are just going on because we happened to be the ones who made it through The Burning, what is the point? Maybe we need the arrogance of believing ourselves special, and good. Maybe not purely good. Only *trying* to be good? Maybe I need to forget the list of negative things I said about myself to Bayat and start to embrace something else?

I wonder what Bayat really thinks of me. What does he really know about me? I still know so little about him. *My* hunter I called him, but really ... Yes, I can picture his brown eyes gazing into me, feel his lips on mine and his hot hand on the back of my neck. Yes, maybe I'm beginning to understand what it is to have someone in your life who feels like everything to you. But is that really the same as *knowing* them?

LETTERS

2

My dear daughter,

I wonder where you are now, what thoughts you are thinking, if you are afraid or feeling vulnerable, if you are, at times, happy. I wish I could get some sense of you. How hard it is to be so completely separated. How strange it is to keep returning to our empty hut, expecting to see you and your father sitting by the fire, talking quietly or laughing uproariously. I wish I could find a memory of you and I laughing but it was always your father keeping us light, warding off my natural tendency towards dark imaginings.

Ever since you were born, I have been scared of what could happen. Here, in the wilderness. You cannot understand how the mud and the trees and the dirt and the open, untouched sky terrified me. How I have had to fight my urge to flee, to ghost, as so many have done, in search of something more.

Yes, Pan, I am one of those and it is only your father, and then you, which has kept me here. I can hardly believe I am confessing to these thoughts. If we survive, and return to our former lives, I think I will have to burn these pages.

In the meantime, more confession. When I ended my last letter, I was back in the laboratory. I hate to think of how weak I was. My whole life had been directed by my parents and, then, Ivan. He was a brilliant man, smarter than anyone I'd ever known, determined and ambitious. He stood a foot taller than me and had long, black hair which he tied back in a ponytail, his one form of non-convention. He was not unkind. He loved me, in his own way, and I loved his intensity.

I said I couldn't say I was noble and good. I can say *I thought* I was being noble and good, for a while.

We were working on a vaccine project around an immunodeficiency virus – H1T3 – which had caused a pandemic years before. The team was led by Ivan, I was second-in-charge and there were three lab assistants: Louise, Mandrake and Hector. We were testing the virus's resistance to high doses of ordinary vitamins. I know most of this science will go over your head, but there might be a day when this comes in handy. We were trying to determine if it could be broken down at all, as none of the conventional drugs were effective. The epidemic had only been controlled through complete isolation of victims: whole communities simply cordoned off and left to die. If H1T3 came back, it could take many more of us before such measures were able to be implemented.

The work was painstaking and disheartening. News would filter through of terrible injuries and deaths from the frequent uprisings outside our gated world and I would long to go out and be a doctor, to actually administer to those who were wounded.

'What we're doing here is just as important,' Ivan would say to me and I tried to believe it. Even more so when we seemed to shift our focus from vitamins to, what I thought, were the already ineffective drug schedules of the past.

'We need to be sure they don't work,' Ivan insisted.

He became more and more absent from the lab and I would find him on the phone – the last of the communication tools left to us – talking confidently to faceless investors about the 'closeness of success'. Ivan needed the money of the drug corporations for our research to continue. They wanted to be the ones to provide the vaccination, to those rich enough to buy it.

'And what about the poor?' I asked when I finally confronted him. I had known for months what we were doing was useless, and still I'd kept on. I can only say it was just easier, Pan, than dealing with the truth. I said I wanted to go 'out there' and help the less fortunate, yet I didn't do it. To be honest, it was just easier to stay behind the locked gates and take care of my own.

'What do I care about the poor?' Ivan countered, and I knew I had kidded myself about him, as much as I had kidded myself about my own heroic desires. 'We need to make money. We can drag these trials on for years if we can just give them an occasional sliver of hope.'

We went on together. I would have fled his cold eyes and ruthless pursuit of fortune, but I had nowhere to run to. I knew I wouldn't survive a day on my own outside the gates.

You might not be able to comprehend this, Pan. This cowardice. This inability to leave what you've always known and plunge into the unknown. In fact, I know you won't understand, given what you are currently doing. You are so much braver than me.

I would have continued on this way until The Burning. I would have been wiped out, like all the rest and you would never have been born, if it hadn't been for that one day in the lab.

Can you picture them again? Rooms of white. Test-tubes and microscopes, petri dishes and vacuum-sealed drawers containing deathly viruses? Computers running simulations? Filing cabinets towering to the ceiling lined with fluorescent lights? A view through the bullet-proof glass to the smoking city around us? I suspect not.

We had always been very careful. Louise, a gangly girl in her early twenties, was known to be extra cautious.

I can still hear her scream.

I was in the corridor, taking a coffee break from testing the drug ZarVex, developed by our newly acquired sponsor, Kaplan pharmaceuticals. I ran in to find Louise lying, face up, on the floor. Next to her was a smashed vial of H1T3.

'Lock down!' I screamed and pushed the red button which set off the whirling screech of the alarm. Immediately, steel shutters began to descend on the windows and the automatic doors started to close, one by one. There were six in all, closing in sequence, giving us the chance to escape. Ivan, who'd been at the computer bank, made it out door number two. Mandrake had already sprinted past me before the third door shut. But where was Hector?

I ran to the fourth door. It was already half shut. I spun around and saw Hector kneeling beside Louise on the floor.

'Get away from her!' I yelled.

He looked up at me and shook his head.

'She's going to die, Hector!' I don't know why I shouted this. It wasn't as if Hector didn't already know it, and Louise curled into a ball and began to sob.

The fourth door shut. I ran to the fifth and, this time, I didn't look back, falling into the corridor.

Ivan and Mandrake were already in the office, watching the closed camera circuit television showing Louise and Hector in the lab. In the grainy black and white I could see he was holding her hand.

So, here is another example of my cowardice. What will you think of your mother, Pan? At least know that I stayed and witnessed. Unlike Ivan and Mandrake, who slunk away, unable to bear Louise's screams and convulsions, the gasping for breath and the final vomit and contortions. It lasted for hours and Hector was there for her, never leaving her side.

He went into quarantine straight after and I visited him every day. I could not talk to him, I could only wave and smile through the glass. Most times, I simply sat in a plastic chair, near the door where, at the very least, he could see me.

They couldn't understand why Hector hadn't contracted the virus or how he had been able to avoid contamination. After two months, though, even Ivan had to concede he wasn't going to get sick and they said he could go.

'Free at last?' I said, standing at his bedside. A pathetic opening line.

'Not until we get out of this place.'

I still remember the thrill which ran through me.

'We?'

He took my hand and gripped it, just as he had Louise's dying fingers. I looked at his black skin interlaced with mine and kissed the back of his palm.

'Always.'

You will have suspected, Pan, that your father is a brave man. Now you know just how brave.

Six weeks later, we made our escape. I wasn't just running away from the iciness of Ivan, I was running *with* the new idea of what a person could be, at their very best.

Hector, like me, had known for a long time our research work was stalling, a charade for duping big business and lining Ivan's pockets. Unlike me, he had been making plans. He was certain things were moving towards disaster and he wanted to get out, as quickly as possible. If we had any doubts, a visit from Louise's twin sister, Kalina, convinced us.

'What kind of facility doesn't have better precautions in place?' Kalina demanded. She had the same thin, pretty face as her sibling, though the set of her jaw was harder and her voice full of an anger we never encountered in Louise. Ivan had granted Kalina's request to see where her sister had died and she stood in the lab, in the exact spot where Louise had fallen to the ground. She had seen the video footage. I watched it with her, as Ivan didn't want it leaving the building. I could barely believe how unmoved she seemed, not turning away during the whole ordeal.

'Thank you for staying with her,' she said to Hector. 'If you ever consider leaving this lab, please be in touch. I work at Chimera and we would value you more highly than this place clearly does.'

Later, Hector told me Chimera was known for experimentation with animal viral vortices and he wanted nothing to do with it. We had heard the rumours of where some of that research was going.

The irony was that Louise's death had actually led

us to a breakthrough. As we could no longer stomach working with H1T3, we tested ZarVex on a series of lesser viruses and found it to be an antibiotic of outstanding abilities. If we had not been so focused on escape, we might have made a change, we might have done something to reverse where everything was headed. We were too selfish, though. Love can do that to you. All we wanted was to get away, to be together.

Don't forget this, Pan. Love can be wonderful, but it doesn't always make you do the right thing.

I have to stop again. This time, it's not because I have to be somewhere, I just don't think I can go into this particular memory right now. Those days were the time when I was the most scared in my life. Hours and hours of terror. This is my only excuse for never talking to you of it. Oh, how I wish you were here with me again. How I wish I could give you a hug and tell you everything is going to be fine. I can only hope you are somewhere safe and that you are all taking care of each other.

All my love,

Zaana

PART THREE

11

The creatures are on the other side of the door. The blood from Matthew's head wound is streaming down his face again. I have no idea where the others are, or if they are even alive. I think in my heart I believed I was special and I would survive, no matter what. Now I know better.

We left the mountains as soon as the sun peeked its head up. We had packed our bags with enough supplies for at least five days.

'Do you think you want to take that?' Emmaline asked. She was pointing at my cloak. 'Isn't it a bit heavy?'

Was she bringing it up because she hated the fact

Bayat had given the cloak to me, a visible sign of his preference for me, over her? I knew she had been humiliated by the pretend-to-be-hurt incident and its lack of outcome. It made sense that she had made a try for Bayat. She didn't have a Chosen and we were all lonely, away from home. But I didn't want to compete with her anymore.

'It keeps me warm, Emmaline.'

'Sure.' She shrugged. 'Your choice.'

I didn't know if I was going to be able to keep up this civility, travelling with her again. In the village and in the tribe, there'd always been more people to put between myself and her. On the road, we'd be back to a small group and my mixed feelings towards Emmaline would be harder to hide. Mind you, this worry turned to nothing when I realised Oyan was coming with us.

Matthew and Titus were waiting on the stone ridge, their bags slung over their shoulders. They didn't look or smell very fresh. I knew I was also pretty pungent. I'd had a chance to wash my face in the river yesterday morning but, in the meantime, had sweated through the exertions of last night. My eyelids felt heavy. Our rest day had disappeared into horror. There was no question of delaying any longer, though. The arrival of the disease had spurred us on again. I didn't want to think about how things had changed once more, as if we were trying to outrun the sickness.

'Are you cold?' Matthew asked, and I realised I had actually quivered in my dread. He stepped toward me, like he was going to put his arms around me.

'No, no.' I pulled the cloak closer. He stopped and, stony faced, turned away.

'You'll be warming up soon enough, river girl,' a voice declared and we all looked around to see Oyan and Bayat, both with rabrat skin bags on their backs, striding down the path from the upper caves. I had no idea how he'd heard our conversation.

This was just the first of Oyan's falsely friendly comments to me. My stomach dropped at the sight of him with a bag and the arrival of Mayhaan a few moments later confirmed the brothers' short time as tribal leaders was over.

Mayhaan was not the same confident man I'd met only five days ago. His back was hunched and his shoulders rounded, as if his all-night vigil with Bettina had permanently weakened his bones. The tufts of hair on his head were flattened and the wrinkles of his face seemed deeper.

We waited. I didn't know who should speak or what should be spoken and, as we crept looks at Mayhaan, he stared away into the distance.

Finally, he shook himself out of his reverie and stood just a bit straighter.

'River People,' he began, in a voice of solemnity, 'you came to the mountains as part of a quest to save your village. We offered you food and shelter and the skills of our greatest hunter.'

Bayat blushed and Oyan scowled.

'Now, your misfortune has visited the Mayhaanan. We do not know if this tragedy has come with you, but we can see finally why you would choose not to give in, why you would journey into danger to find help for those you love. We can only be grateful for your knowledge and your courage and send with you the two tribesmen who may help you succeed.'

'Thank you, Mayhaan,' I said. Though it had been directed to all of us, I knew Mayhaan remembered my argument with him, his reference to understanding was his way of apologising for his former dismissal of our plan.

We shook hands with Mayhaan and a few of the other tribespeople who were taking a break from their nursing duties, and started down the path we had taken every morning since our arrival, towards the training field. As I looked back and waved at Mayhaan, I thought of how hard it is to care about people you have never met, how Mayhaan wished for our return only because of the threat to Bettina and his own tribe. Was this how our parents were before The Burning? Looking out for those they knew, turning their back on those they didn't? In a world of thousands, maybe that's all they could do …

From my position behind Emmaline and Matthew, I couldn't actually tell if it was Bayat or Oyan who was leading because, from the back, they looked exactly the same. Matthew kept looking around, checking I was all right, whilst Bayat never turned his head.

Behind me, Titus and Fatima were whenever possible walking side by side. Fatima's ankle had healed enough to walk without limping, although I noticed her tendency to try to avoid putting all her weight on it. Her face had only the remnants of her wounds and I'd also noticed a change between her and Titus. They were always together now. Not openly affectionate, just sitting close if they got the chance and naturally staying near one another.

As we came to the turn-off to the training field, I half expected to trundle down to the grass sacks and knife piles. But, of course, the knives were now in our bags, and we had picked up our bows and quivers of arrows at the ridge.

So we continued on, following a dirt track through the lower mountain until we were, once again, alongside the river. On both banks, oak trees lined the vista as far as the eye could see, a valley of deep green.

With the weapons and the cloak and the bag, I was, like Oyan had predicted, warmed up in a very short time. The day was bright and windy and I was grateful again for our escape from the stench of sickness. The water babbled beside us and the forest waved its branches at us, as if hurrying us along. I didn't have the same wonder I had felt upon first leaving the village, and I was too aware of how quickly fatigue and irritation would come to me from continuous walking, but I still couldn't help enjoying this beginning time, when my legs felt strong and the heat of my feet could be abated with a simple splash into the stream.

Bayat had told us the first day would be relatively easy, as we travelled west we could stay along the edge of the river without too much difficulty. It was only when it took a turn to the south, we would begin to struggle. He had not given us too many details, I suspected he didn't want to dishearten us, only saying that the terrain after this was 'challenging'.

I didn't want to think ahead or, really, behind. For just this time I wanted to be where I was, drinking in the strange solitude of trekking with six other people, concentrating on each step, finding the gentlest path for my toes. Matthew wanted to guide me, sometimes I followed his route, sometimes I went my own way.

Of course, it's all very well to imagine you're not going to think about the future, or the past. Much harder to actually do it. The night had brought back horrible memories: that panicked search in the hall for my parents; Hildur's stiff body as it was lowered into the ground; little Hope crying for her mother.

To drive these thoughts away, I tried to think about what might happen. Bayat had said we'd go through our strategy when we came to the outskirts of the city. He'd rightly assumed we were all too tired this morning to truly take in any detailed ideas. So, really, everything that lay before me was a bit of a blank. For some reason, every time I tried to picture the creatures, all I could see was the cougar's face, snarling.

'Do you want me to take your bag for a while?' Matthew had dropped back to walk beside me. He had his hat in one hand and ruffled up his hair with the other.

I knew his offer to take my bag was him being kind. I still found it annoying, as if he thought I was too weak to cope.

'No, I'm doing fine, thanks.'

'You don't have to be so proud, Pan. You can let people in sometimes. I know your shoulder is still hurting from the cat attack.'

I had to admit the effect of Bettina's cream had worn off quickly. Or was it Bayat's touch?

'I'm not being proud, I'm just being myself.'

This was what Matthew had never been able to get. Our moments of friction weren't me being unreasonable, they were just me being who I was.

Matthew stayed silent. He glanced over his shoulder and I followed his gaze to see Fatima and Titus, a fair way back, strolling together, holding hands. Titus had Fatima's bag slung over one shoulder and his own over the other, making him sway from side to side.

'I guess Fatima's leg will be feeling this,' I said, trying to account for *her* ability to let someone else in, to not be so proud.

'Sometimes…' Matthew began. We were still walking side by side. He was looking out across the river, to the far bank where the darkness of the forest seemed more sinister, full of distant dangers. Whatever comfort I'd got from being on 'our' side had gone.

'Sometimes …' Matthew started again. 'I think you don't even like me anymore.'

The words came out in a rush, like he'd had to force them through his teeth.

I felt queasy. Why did he have to do this?

'Of course I like you.' I wanted to make the conversation light and breezy. 'We've been friends for forever.'

'Friends.' He repeated the word like I'd just fired a direct arrow into his heart.

'You know me better than anyone.' I wasn't sure if this was totally true, but I needed to give him something.

'Yeah, I do.'

He stopped walking and so I did too. He was still threading the edge of his hat in his hands. I had seen him do this so often, a nervous habit whenever he was stressed or unsure of himself.

'I know you think ...' he began again and trailed off. 'You think I'm just following the village rules, but I'm not. If they'd told me anyone else was my Chosen, I wouldn't have accepted it. I've always wanted it to be you, Pan. You're honest and sensitive and strong, and you've always been there for me. I care for you so much, I want to look after you even though I know you don't want me to. Even though I know ...'

I had been concentrating on his feet, completely unable to meet his eyes. I couldn't really believe he was saying these things. Words that, only the day before, I'd so desperately wanted to hear from Bayat.

I looked up to see he was fixated on a point further down the path. When I followed his gaze again, I saw Emmaline, Oyan and Bayat, all stopped, watching Matthew and me. They were too far ahead to be able to hear what Matthew had been saying, though I suspected Oyan would be making some suggestions. I knew my face was red; I could feel heat in every part of it.

'I'm not as glamorous as ...' Matthew whispered. 'But I know you, Pan. I know you.'

The day wore on. Even though I'd known it would come, the fatigue of having to walk and walk and walk crept up so slowly I didn't really know how tired I was until Bayat called us to a halt and declared we would set up camp for the night. The shock of suddenly stopping, of lifting off the weight of the bow and the quiver of arrows and the bag and the cloak, of letting my legs squat down and falling backwards onto the bed of cleared ground Bayat had found for us, was almost enough to make me cry with relief. I didn't though, too aware of watching eyes.

All during the rest of the day's travel, I'd had Matthew's words in my head and Bayat's body in my sight. Unlike the morning, Bayat had frequently turned to look over his shoulder and, although he never looked directly at me – most often he did an exaggerated scan of us, as if checking on our relative positions – I could sense his renewed interest in my whereabouts. I didn't know why, but this riled me even more than when he hadn't bothered looking behind.

In the bustle of setting up the fire and trying to wash and eat before the sun went down, I was easily able to avoid speaking to anyone. My head was overloaded with questions and fears and confusions and I couldn't wait to lie down and mull them all over in the quiet and peace of pre-sleep.

As always, it seemed someone else had other ideas.

'I know everyone is tired,' Bayat began. We had just finished our dinner. 'But I need to talk to you about the time ahead. I want you to have my plans and ideas inside your minds for the next few days. I want you to think about them all the time, and come up with problems and things we might need to change.'

Despite my exhaustion, there was something about the way he spoke which sent a thrill through me. He sounded so alive, strong and passionate. Yes, he was definitely glamorous.

It's embarrassing to admit, but even though I looked intently at him, I hardly understood what he said. His descriptions of the landscape and how things would be so different when we left the river and the forest behind were too strange. This talk of steel and concrete and glass. I knew metal from the blade of a knife but there was no way I could truly imagine it making places to live or bridges to cross the water. Nor did the other substances make any sense to me.

Besides, how could I think about the days ahead when I still had Matthew's declaration of love swimming around inside me? He had said everything I'd wanted to hear from Bayat: he'd told me about what I was to him and how he saw me. Maybe my parents had got it right. Maybe Fatima was right.

We have a responsibility. To our people. To the land.

I watched Bayat's lips move, still not able to focus properly on the words. The others were murmuring and nodding. They all seemed to think his plan, of which I had no real idea, was fine. I would just have to trust them.

The next day was almost exactly the same as the first. We rose early and began trekking in the same order: Bayat, Oyan, Emmaline, Matthew, me, Titus and Fatima. The forest still stayed conveniently back from the river, and we simply walked along the bank, only occasionally having to skirt around boulders or the bracken we'd encountered in the first days of our journey.

After lunch, Titus and Fatima dropped completely out of sight.

'Maybe someone should go back and check they haven't hurt themselves,' I suggested when we all noticed.

Oyan smirked at me.

'I'm sure they're getting along just fine,' he said.

When they caught up much later, I tried to get a good look at Fatima, to see if there were any visible signs of her crossing into that other land, the place I'd yet to go with anyone. I couldn't see it, though. She looked the same as she had for the last two days, since she and Titus had got together, flushed and smugly happy but not … totally different. Wouldn't it show? Wouldn't it be completely obvious?

That evening I splashed water on my face down at the river's edge – Bayat had skilfully chosen a spot near a ford which, in the morning, would allow us all to have a proper bath – and scrubbed at the layer of dirt which had begun to accumulate behind my ears. How disgusted my mother would be, to see the muck coming away under my fingernails. She had always been so diligent about my cleaning habits, almost obsessive.

Thinking of her, I searched amongst the stones for a piece of charcoal. I had one in my bag but the effort of going back to find it was too much.

'Have you lost something, Babbler?'

I glanced up. Oyan stood a few feet behind me. I

hadn't heard him approach, I guess he wasn't as bad a hunter as I'd thought.

'My name is Pan.'

I tried not to show my nerves. I turned my back on him, picking up a small black fragment and rubbing it over my teeth. The dryness of the charcoal made my lips shrivel up.

'I wonder what my brother sees in you.'

He had moved closer. As I stood, I realised he was just behind me.

'We've always been very different.' He was breathing on my neck. 'But maybe we can share something …'

I smelt blood, it must've been coming from him, the faint remnant of past hunts. Something about this reminded me of the cougar and her strong, shining eyes. I spun around and kneed him hard, right between the legs.

He cried out in pain, doubling over.

The others came running, probably expecting another encounter with a wild animal.

'What's going on?' Bayat asked, putting his arm around his twin's shoulder. I suppose it shouldn't have surprised me to see him go immediately to his brother's side, rather than to me. 'Pandora?'

'What happened?' Matthew asked, although he didn't come close.

I spat the charcoal into the water. I squatted down and rinsed out my mouth. A moment before, it had seemed the best thing to do, to hurt Oyan before he hurt me. Now, I was shaky, trying to avoid Bayat's accusing eyes.

'I wasn't doing anything ...' Oyan whined.

'He ... hurt himself,' I said to Bayat and strode away, back to the fire.

I knew now that Oyan was dangerous and I would have to keep away from him. I hadn't done anything to deserve his hatred and could only put it down to jealousy of his brother who Mayhaan and the rest of the tribe so clearly preferred to him.

Across from me, in the firelight, I could make out the outline of Titus and Fatima, their bodies curled into one another, just like my mother and father had always slept. Oyan and Bayat were lying a little further over, next to each other, though not touching. Emmaline lay near my feet. Matthew was hidden by the glowing logs. I rolled onto my back and looked up at the lonely stars.

<h1 style="text-align:center">12</h1>

Nothing could've got me ready for the sight of the bridge. In our lessons, there had been books – a random collection of now-mildewed volumes in our hotchpotch library – so we had seen photos of skyscrapers and towns. These, though, were small and fuzzy. They looked kind of flimsy and there was no way to imagine them towering above you, like the three humped structure did.

It was as if it had come out of nowhere. One moment we were stumbling through the undergrowth because we'd hit the 'challenging' terrain at last, and the ground sloped hopelessly down towards the river, trying to push us in. We'd been sweating and cursing our way along for half the day, Fatima complaining to me that the bath she'd had in the morning hadn't been worth it since she was so hot and revolting already. I didn't say how I'd been too worried about encountering Oyan to risk undressing.

The stately trees had morphed into broken, scratching bushes, leaf litter crunching beneath our feet. Plus stone ridges we had to struggle over, often throwing our bags ahead of us to make the scramble possible.

I was actually still contemplating my bleeding big toe from the last of these horrible climbs when I heard Fatima gasp.

'Oh. *By the rivers ...*'

And there it was. As I said, it had three humps, each criss-crossed with steel beams and held up with great slabs of what I knew must be concrete. We were only a few feet away from the first of these, stepping into the mud it arose from. Bayat and Oyan stood next to what they called a pylon, both leaning on it, as if testing its strength.

When I stared up at the stars and thought I was small, it was the endless sky making me feel it. Now it was this thing, so not-endless, so completely *finished*. I tried to remember it had been made by people. Like our mud-brick huts, it had been built. Except, I had no idea how such a thing would have been put together. With our homes, it was brick by brick. How had this thing held itself up when only half done? How had it reached out across the water when there was nothing below to support it? Why didn't it fall apart?

'Ow! Pan!' In my awe, I had grabbed Fatima's arm and was squeezing her wrist with my fingers.

'Sorry.' I let go.

We both kept staring.

'My father used to sing me a song when I was young about a bridge that was falling down.' Fatima's voice had the threat of tears. 'I could never really understand what it meant.'

'You can tell him about it when we get back,' I said, trying to sound certain. 'How you understand now.'

'I suppose.' But her voice had the same doubt in it I felt.

The seven of us gathered at the base, caught in the shadow of the great bridge.

'We'll sit and rest in the shade for a bit,' Bayat ordered. 'From now on we'll be pretty exposed.'

I squatted down at the far end of the pylon, away from the others, leaning my back against the cold concrete. It was so strong, not a chance of it giving way. I pivoted and ran my hand down the coarse greyness. What would it have been like to live surrounded by this stuff? The vastness of the bridge already freaked me out. How would I cope with the rest of the city?

'You get used to it.' Bayat squatted down beside me, also facing the pylon.

'The bridge … it just seems not from our world.'

'Yes.'

'But I guess it is … from our world.'

'Just not the one you know.'

'Do you … do you want to know about this other world?' I asked, thinking of how much I'd always wanted to leave the village.

'I was born five years before the End, Pandora. I have some … memories.'

I realised I have made him younger than he was. He was twenty-five notches on the Growing Tree.

'What was it like back then?' I knew I sounded too eager.

'They aren't good memories.'

He didn't say anything more.

'But what about now?' I asked, finally. 'What kind of worlds do you think are out here?'

'I've been hunting away from the tribe all my life, Pandora. I've gone further than anyone else. But I still don't know what's really out there. *Who's* really out there. None of us do.'

'Have you ever thought about ... ghosting?'

He shook his head. 'We have stories in the tribe ... Those who wander never come back for a reason,' he said. 'Maybe they returned to the city and were killed by the ferals. Or maybe there's something worse out there.'

'Or, maybe ...' I knew I had to finally speak the secret hope I had harboured in my heart so long. '... There is a place where the new world has begun.'

Bayat frowned.

'What do you mean?'

I was disappointed he didn't understand straight away.

'Our elders never told us the whole story of The Burning, certainly not about these creatures. What else didn't they tell us? What else might they not know about? What else, who else, might we find?'

Bayat wasn't looking at me any longer, his gaze had gone off into the distance, maybe some other place where his loved ones were.

'There might be ... *thousands* ... of others.' The word felt strange on my tongue, yet I couldn't let it go.

Bayat fixed his eyes back on me. He didn't look

happy, as if the momentary fantasy had made him angry.

'We need to concentrate on those who we have, Pandora, not on your imaginary thousands. You told me you wondered if you'd left your village for the right reasons. You need to remember what we are here for.'

He stood. I was stung. He thought I was just a silly child, dreaming of silly things. I should never have told him my secret longings. He was judging me. He thought I didn't care. What did he know? What did he even know about me anyway?

It was time to tell him the whole truth.

'Bayat, when we get back to the village, I am Matthew's Chosen, which means we are expected to live and … breed together, for the rest of our lives.'

There, I had finally told him. He would understand how our time together was limited, how we were doomed lovers.

'Yes, I know, Pandora. Emmaline told me the day you hurt her knee.'

He started to walk away, to where the rest of them sat talking, before turning back to me.

'Thank you for telling me. At last.'

All this time, he had known. When he ran his fingers along my scars, he had known. When he watched Matthew speaking to me, he had known.

At least, he hadn't known when he had kissed me.

Is that why he hadn't tried again? I could believe it. But what did that mean? That he cared I was chosen for another? Or that he didn't actually care for me? Maybe this was just a game to him. Too many times I couldn't see his feelings for me. Too many times he turned to stone.

Maybe there were parts of him like his brother. My stomach squirmed at the idea of it. Surely, he was nothing like his twin? He had never tried to force himself onto me. If anything, he had held back. But was this just because of knowing about Matthew? *By the rivers*, I was confused.

And I knew this wasn't what I should be thinking about. He was right about one thing, I needed to remember what we were here for.

We climbed up onto the concrete road – Bayat named it a highway – and followed it through a series of hills and valleys. Twenty years had passed since it was used by cars and yet it seemed not to have changed, there were a few cracks, but mostly it remained smooth and easy to walk on, only smarting our feet a little with the heat. Four lanes running alongside each other. Bayat pointed out the faded white lines which had marked the channels for each traveller so, for the first time, we could walk in a horizontal line, side by side.

But we didn't.

Bayat and Oyan still strode ahead of the rest of us, not exactly next to one another, but close enough. Emmaline and Matthew followed alongside each other, with Matthew occasionally dropping back to try to be alongside me, although I kept dropping back from him, determined not to give him the chance to talk to me again. I wanted silence.

Titus and Fatima held hands and strolled along behind me, as if we were going on some summer amble through the forest. I wanted to remind them of how serious our venture was but, then again, I saw how much happier Fatima looked and couldn't blame them for finding solace in one another. Constant misery wasn't going to help any of us.

We passed through great slabs of pale yellow, crumbling rock, the road cutting through as if whoever had built it couldn't be bothered taking a sidestep. Without the shade of trees, we were grateful for these overhanging cliffs. They gave us a bit of shade. Otherwise, we were directly in the sun. For once, I envied Matthew's hat, though I shook my head at his offer for me to wear it.

'You'll be burnt in no time without it,' I insisted and he shrugged.

'Let me know if you change your mind.'

I was surprised at this willingness to give up the point. Maybe he was finally starting to get sick of me. I couldn't blame him.

My bag was heavy and so was Bayat's cloak, and the string of the bow kept digging into the skin on the side of my neck. If Matthew had offered to carry it now, I might have stopped being so proud. Only this time, he didn't.

We stopped for lunch in the relative coolness of one of the split-open mountains, with a view of the next and, according to Bayat, last bridge we would cross before catching sight of the city. This bridge was held up by impossibly long, thin steel ropes, dipping down like the curve of a bowl, and hung over a huge ravine. From where we sat we were yet to see its bottom and I already felt anxious about having to cross it, not only because of how high it was but because it meant we would soon be in reach of the ferals. Soon, our training would be tested in this new, too-real world.

I sat a little bit away from the others again. I couldn't look at Bayat. I chewed on bread – we had finished our cougar meat the day before – and tried to ignore the rumbling of my always-hungry stomach. I drank some water and leant back against a rock. Its coolness eased my sweating back. I tried not to breathe in too deeply, I didn't want to get a mouthful of my own stink. I wet my fingertips and, closing my eyes, dabbed my forehead and cheeks.

'Would you like me to blow on you, to cool you off?'

Oyan squatted down next to me. I inched away, trying to make sure his skin couldn't make contact with mine.

'Just leave me alone, Oyan.'

'That's not very friendly.'

'Why would I be friendly to you?' My voice was shaky.

'My brother isn't who you think he is, you know,' his voice had dropped to a whisper. He glanced over his shoulder to where Bayat and the others sat, eating and talking, it seemed, happily. 'He isn't as chivalrous as everyone likes to believe. I know things. Things he's done.'

His blue-green eyes shone malevolently and he had a grin on his face which, if not for his similarity to Bayat, would have made him a monster before me.

'I don't care.' I tried to sound convincing, although even I couldn't help being curious. 'I don't care about your stories and I don't care about your brother!'

As soon as I said it, I knew they'd be listening. Sure enough, they'd all fallen silent at the exact moment I spoke. The words seemed to echo down the highway, tumbling along the grey road, catching at the ghosts who floated there.

I walked in the centre of the bridge, refusing to go near the edges and look down into the chasm below. Emmaline shouted at me from the side, gripping hold of the steel barriers and leaning over, down into the wind.

'You should come see this!'

I stayed with Fatima who, like me, didn't have much curiosity to witness just how ridiculously high we were from the ground. The boys were whooping and mucking around, shoving each other into the metal mesh, climbing up the poles dotted along the barricades, yelling into the heated air, running down the arching roadway. For once, Fatima was holding my hand, Titus was busy being an idiot, and we were in the same kind of mood.

'I wish they wouldn't do that. It's really dangerous,' Fatima said, sounding just like her mother.

'Yeah, it's pretty dumb.'

Fatima glanced at me. We were almost half way across the bridge. Our arms swung together, like we were young ones again. The wind our enemy, pushing into our backs, forcing us to tense our legs on the downward slope.

'I expected you to tell me to stop being so fussy. That they need to let off steam.'

I knew those words had been on the tip of my tongue. This time, I'd tried to see it from Fatima's point of view.

'What would I know, Fatima?' I sighed. 'Every time I speak I seem to hurt someone.'

I was on the verge of tears.

'Bayat knows you didn't mean it.'

'Does he?'

'You two ...'

'Yes?'

I desperately wanted Fatima to tell me what Bayat

and I were. To make sense of what I couldn't. We had begun the upward ascent, the wind our friend, helping us along.

'There's something weird between the two of you.'

'Weird?'

No, this wasn't what I wanted to hear.

'I don't know how to describe it, Pan. Like a vibe, except I cannot tell if it is because you really like one another, or you really don't …'

'Great.'

'And then there is Matthew.'

This was going from bad to worse. Fatima's point of view turned out to be exactly what I didn't want to hear right now.

'I think we should stop talking about this, Fat.' I didn't need another reminder of how much Fatima loved Matthew and how I should too.

'Fine, Pan.' I was surprised by her willingness to change subjects, until I realised what she actually wanted to talk about. 'What do you think about me and Titus?'

'Um, what do you mean?'

'Don't you think it's just …?'

She had become fluttery. We were at the end of the bridge. I stopped walking, dropped her hand.

'Yeah, I suppose.'

'Did I tell you how it happened? It was that day I came to training for the first time. I mean, he had been paying me heaps more attention ever since ... well, after I got hurt he was really kind and helpful.'

I didn't mention this was probably because he felt so guilty, after running away and leaving her to be attacked by a cougar. That wouldn't have been tactful.

'You wouldn't have noticed how he kept on getting my food and asking me if I was comfortable and so many other little things. Anyway, on that day I came down to the field and you tried to show me how to fire an arrow. You were so distracted, it was totally hopeless.'

The day Bayat had taken Emmaline back to the caves after I hurt her. The day Bayat was told Matthew was my Chosen.

'So, once you'd gone for your run, Titus came to help me. He'd put his arms around me, to show me how to hold it.'

He had used the same moves as Bayat. Had Titus watched and learnt it from him? Training in more things than fighting?

'Pan, it was just so ... I don't even know how to describe it.'

'You don't have to.'

On her face was the same smile as mine, as I remembered Bayat's skin against me.

We giggled.

'That night, when we were about to separate after dinner, he kissed me on the cheek. And, the next morning, he took my hand and, then, he gave me a proper, tongue kiss when ...'

'Okay, okay. I don't need the gory details.'

Fatima's face fell in disappointment.

'Don't you?'

The truth was jealousy had kicked in. And, despite my sort-of happiness for Fatima, I still wasn't convinced Titus's change of attitude to her came from the right place. Had she forgotten the way he'd talked to her before? I couldn't let it pass.

'What has he actually said to you?'

'What do you mean?'

'About why he likes you? About why he wants to suddenly be with you?'

Fatima frowned.

We were still waiting for the others to catch up. All their bravado had been screamed out, and the four boys were trudging up towards us, with Emmaline a fair way behind. The wind smacked at their clothes and bags.

'He doesn't have to say anything. Actions speak louder than words.'

I wouldn't say how Titus's actions hadn't exactly spoken much for his bravery or how he hadn't acted particularly well to her throughout most of his life. I understood now I had to say what Fatima wanted to hear.

'You're right,' I said and hugged her. 'I'm really happy for you.'

She returned the embrace.

'Thanks, Panda.'

Maybe I could be a big, sweet bear.

Crossing the bridge had released something in everyone and we took the next summit as a straight line, shoulder to shoulder. I had Matthew on one side and Fatima on the other and, despite all that had happened and was bound to happen, I was pleased to be amongst my people, these two who I'd grown up with, who'd seen the same sights as me, who knew how precious the village was we were trying to save.

At the top of the mountain, in the far distance, we saw the city for the first time.

It wasn't much.

I suppose I'd expected it to be huge, like the towering pylons of the bridge. Instead, it was a glimmer on the horizon, a dot of cleared land at the end of the snaking road. There were no buildings projecting into the sky, no glint of vertical glass, just a mass of rubble.

'Most of the skyscrapers came down in the blasts,' Bayat explained, as if sensing our disappointment. 'The ones that survived are too far away to see from here. And some of the larger buildings are still intact too. You'll see when we get closer.'

It was as if he was apologising, as if it was his fault our first glimpse hadn't been interesting or awe-inspiring enough.

'We're not here to see the sights,' I said, hoping to reassure him.

'I didn't say you were,' he retorted. 'I was just explaining how things are.'

He sounded colder than he ever had. More like Oyan.

'Where are we going to camp?' Fatima asked. She gave me a quick pat on the arm and I knew she was trying to diffuse whatever was going on with me and Bayat.

'There's a way off the road, over here,' Bayat directed us, his voice becoming a little softer.

We followed the dirt track for a short period and came to a rectangular clearing, marked out with pine logs. Here, we were even higher than we'd been on the highway and the city winked in the distance, seeming further away. Bayat said it was another one and half day's travel, though I couldn't imagine covering so much ground in such a short time. I could only hope we were strong enough.

I couldn't sleep. I snuck away from where the others lay, following the track back down to the highway. I stood on the road, looking again to where the city lay. With the moon three-quarters full, there were dancing shadows everywhere you looked. The land ahead was a dark mass of black, ominous shapes.

Bayat had gone over the plan again around the campfire and this time I listened hard. We were going to split up into pairs and search different sections of Melney for a hospital, the most likely place where the drug would be stored. Though none of us had ever seen one before, we knew enough to be able to identify the right kind of building. Bayat said there would be a symbol on it somewhere and then he made two marks in the dirt with a stick: +. He said the most important thing was not to make unnecessary noise and engage with the ferals. I wanted to ask him

why he didn't call them 'creatures', like Mayhaan
had. I was too nervous of him, though. I didn't want
my head bitten off again. The first trip in would be
purely scouting, absolutely no combat until we were
all together.

The thought of sneaking through this unknown
place – avoiding people transformed into beasts –
wouldn't fall out of my brain. I paced back and forth.

'Can't you sleep?'

A figure walked down the track. A Bayat-Oyan
shaped figure. I couldn't tell from the voice which
one of them it was, and tensed at the idea of being
alone again with Oyan.

'Pandora ... I'm sorry about before.'

I relaxed a bit, knowing it was only Bayat who
used my full name. I didn't completely relax, though,
because it wasn't as if things were all that easy
between us. He was apologising, sure. Was that
enough? I wanted everything to be good again,
like it had been, so briefly. But what about Oyan's
words? Hinting that he'd 'done things'? Should I just
completely forget about them?

'I'm sorry, too,' I said. 'I'm sorry I didn't tell you
about Matthew.'

'I'm sorry about my brother.'

'I'm sorry I said I didn't care.'

I could see his face now, his brown eyes glistening in the moonlight. He put his hand up to touch my cheek. It reminded me of the vision I'd had after the cougar attack. Thankfully this time he didn't transform into a great cat, but I still felt a tinge of wariness.

'We're both just really sorry,' I joked, trying not to turn hot at his touch.

'Total sad sacks.'

I was breathing heavily, even though I didn't want to, didn't want it to be so obvious how much I wanted him to kiss me, how off-the-planet I felt when he was so close. Why didn't I? What made me so afraid to show him how much I cared? Was this what Matthew was talking about, that I didn't know how to let people in?

'Are you all right?'

I shook my head.

'I don't know what I am anymore. If I ever have ...'

'You're ... amazing.'

He leant in and our lips joined.

We were hungry for one another, our tongues pushing into each other's mouths, our hands running up and down our bodies. It was different from the first time, when it had all been so new. Now, I knew I didn't want him to stop. I wanted to keep on going until we went to the place I'd only dreamt of. I wanted to be part of him.

This time, it was Bayat who stopped us. We were on the ground by now, the concrete cool and hard against my back. I had my arms above my head, my hands locked with his, his knees on either side of my thighs. He kept dipping down to kiss me on the lips, then drawing back, panting.

'We shouldn't do this,' he said. Then he came down to me again, pushing against me. I couldn't stop myself from groaning with the pleasure of it. How could we not do this?

'This isn't the right time,' he whispered in my ear, trying to convince himself. I wrapped my legs around him. We kissed again and I could feel his hardness.

'We might die in the next few days,' I murmured. 'This is exactly the right time.'

He looked down at me.

'Are you sure?'

A moment before, I'd been completely sure, certain this was what I wanted. His hesitation made me rethink. A break from the heated moment and I suddenly realised the reality of what I would be agreeing to. It wasn't just this tumbling together. It wasn't just kissing and groping and fumbling. It'd be Bayat inside me. Aside from all the awkwardness – I really had no idea of how the act was done, I'd only ever heard my parents doing it, never seen how it all played out – I'd been told by my mother there might be pain, and blood. I knew I didn't want that right now.

Oh, my mother. Was she sitting alone in our hut at this moment, worrying about me?

'Pandora?'

'You're right.' My body was still pulsing. Now there was something else. A kind of calmness. 'This isn't what we should do right now.'

Bayat sighed. He swung off me and sat, wrapping his arms around his knees.

'I was so hoping you weren't going to say that.'

I pushed myself up.

'Then why did you stop and ask if I was sure?' I hoped I didn't sound petulant. 'You could've just kept going, you know.'

'I know.'

I wasn't blaming him, exactly. It just felt easier to make it his fault.

Bayat took a deep breath.

'Whatever you think of Mayhaan, Pandora, he

has been like a father to me. When my brother and I were ... abandoned by our parents, he took us in and raised us, almost like his own. He taught me always to treasure those you love, to try to bring out the best in them. Not to make them do things they might later regret.'

I reached out my hand and ran it through his hair.

'Maybe I wouldn't regret it?' I said in a small voice.

'If you weren't Matthew's Chosen, it would be different.'

The mention of Matthew's name seemed to change the air. It was like I could feel him there, sitting between Bayat and me, like I could hear his declaration of love. *I know you, Pan, I know you.* He was right. He did know me better than Bayat. Did that mean I should be with him? Before, I thought I could dismiss him, I was so sure we would only be together because that was what my parents wanted. Now, I wasn't as confident. What exactly did Bayat and I have, except all this ... heat?

'We should go and get some sleep.' Bayat stood and offered me his hand. He pulled me from the ground and we embraced. My head on his shoulder, I felt his strong arms around me. I wished it wasn't all so complicated.

13

We walked along the highway the next day again, following the dips and curves, although without having to face any more ravines. I guess it was because of the night before, I felt light again, as if nothing could get me down. Stupid, really. It wasn't as if anything had been solved or sorted by my time with Bayat. Matthew still sat on my horizon and Oyan still hovered as a menacing threat, with his mysterious stories. Only knowing Bayat cared for me and wanted me – he thought I was amazing – seemed to make everything better, even if only for a little while.

It did make me think about Emmaline once more, and her lack of a Chosen. I had forgotten about it, with everything happening. Feeling happier again, with this new-found sense of how I was connected to both Matthew and Bayat, even if it was confusing,

I couldn't help wondering about her. And worrying for her. How was she coping knowing she might not have her father when she returned, and had no one else to rely on in the future? I knew I'd never been a real friend and after the stunt she had pulled with her hurt knee, I couldn't imagine ever being her friend, but I could still feel for her. Maybe this was another part of growing up: to see past myself and actually start thinking about how other people might be feeling.

This was my magnanimous phase. It lasted about half a day.

The best thing about walking on hot concrete was its smoothness, not like travelling under the trees, the ground covered in sharp twigs and prickling leaves. The worst thing about walking on hot concrete was its smoothness felt like a flat, hot stone against the skin of your feet, step after step, like being lightly branded, again and again.

To distract myself, I tried to take more notice of the landscape we were passing through. Although at first it seemed to be exactly the same as we'd travelled in before, I realised it wasn't. The closer we got to the city, the shorter, and I assumed younger, the trees were, and the soil in which they grew had sprinklings of black all around, like soot. No noises in the undergrowth because there really wasn't any undergrowth. A few times we saw patches of land where nothing appeared to have grown at all since … well, since The Burning I suppose: big chunks of blackened dirt amongst the struggling, stunted saplings. I could hardly understand how the plants could not have recovered after all this time. I couldn't really get my head around what could leave behind such long-term destruction.

I had a sudden memory of Theodore's careful instructions regarding crop rotation, the importance he placed on allowing ground to recover.

'If there is one thing we have to conquer from the past it is our tendency towards greed.' I remembered him standing in the Great Hall, giving one of his weekly speeches. 'Only grow as much as we need. Let the soil have time to rest, and then sing again.'

I was there, stifling a yawn at the back of the hall, shooting dagger looks at Emmaline, sitting up straight at the very front, nodding in agreement. *By the rivers*, she was so … good. Even my memories didn't help me forgive her.

I had been blinded by the noon sun for a while,

walking with my arm raised in front of my eyes and only now, as the light dipped, did I register where we all were in relation to one another. Bayat, Titus and Matthew were ahead of Fatima and me. Where were the others? I turned back. Oyan and Emmaline were a long way behind, walking side-by-side and quietly talking to one another.

Emmaline and Oyan?

My magnanimity dropped off me like a cloak.

That night – the night before we would enter the city – I didn't leave the camp and fell asleep almost as soon as my head hit the ground. In my dreams, the cougar was stalking me through a silent forest. I could hear her growling, always behind me, though I could not see her. I knew I had to keep on moving, to search for my mother, lost somewhere amongst the empty trees. When I tried to call out to her, though, I could no longer speak. I had become the cat, prowling through the darkness. Hunting. But hunting for what? My mother? Myself? The cougar? I shook my head, trying to clear it of the confusion. My head was too heavy and I had to lie down, my four legs stretched out on the forest floor, my tail twitching like the last movements of a dead thing.

I woke up and touched my face with my hand. For a moment, I had expected to feel fur.

The city was near. We walked all morning, only stopping once for a short rest. Though Emmaline and Oyan were not walking together, I noticed them exchanging looks every now and then. We'd stopped talking hours before, travelling in silence, thinking our separate thoughts. Even Fatima and Titus walked separately and I noticed Fatima's face no longer had the smile she'd been wearing yesterday. There were bags under her eyes. Maybe her dreams had also been filled with strange transformations.

The sky above had turned white with huge grey clouds gathering on the horizon. Every part of my body was tense, as if I'd become one big convoluted knot. I had to constantly stop myself from sipping from my water flask, knowing I needed to conserve it, but was too aware of my dry lips and the soreness of my throat from too much anxious swallowing.

'Here,' Bayat said, stopping. His voice sounded loud after so much quiet. 'This is it.'

A two-lane road split sharply up off the highway

and at the top we could see the first suburban buildings. I felt a strange tingling at the realisation I would be seeing the world my parents had once lived in. The shattered remains of their past.

'As I've said, we'll go in all together, then split into pairs when we reach the harbour.'

'You haven't actually told us who the pairs are going to be.' Oyan spoke with his usual aggression, although I had to admit he did have a point.

'And since there are seven of us, it'll have to be two, two and three, anyway,' Emmaline added, in the same kind of tone as Oyan.

'Right. Sure.' Bayat was reluctant for some reason. 'It'll be Titus and Fatima, Pandora and me, and Oyan, Emmaline and Matthew.'

Now I knew why he'd been hesitating.

'You've got to be kidding,' Oyan muttered.

'No way,' Matthew said at the same time.

'I think that's the most efficient division,' Bayat insisted.

'Efficient? I don't care what you think is efficient,' Matthew snapped. 'I'm going with Pan, no matter what you say, mountain boy.'

I looked down at my feet. The big toe of my left foot had a fresh cut in it I couldn't remember getting.

'Mountain boy?' Bayat echoed. I was waiting for the first punch to fly.

It all seemed unreal. When had I cut my toe?

'I'll go with Matthew,' I said, as quietly as I could.

'I can't go!' Fatima suddenly screamed. 'I can't go at all!'

We all turned to find her squatted on the ground, shaking.

'I really can't go and fight those creatures. I can't! Please don't make me. I thought I was going to be all right. I did. But now … Titus, don't make me. Please.'

Titus looked down at her. I saw a flash of the old disgust he had once shown towards her. It was so quick, though, I might have imagined it. He knelt and put his arm around her.

'Of course we won't make you, Fatima. You can stay here. Don't worry.'

Did Titus really feel this compassion or was he still trying to make up for his own cowardice? What did he really want to say to Fatima? Did he, like me, want to tell her to find her strength, to stop thinking about her needs, her fears, even her death? That now was the time to prove if you were here for yourself or for your people …

'Well, that makes it easier, anyway,' Oyan said, looking down at Fatima with open contempt. 'Titus and Bayat, Emmaline and me, Pan and Matthew.'

Bayat stared at me. I nodded hesitantly.

14

I hugged Fatima goodbye.

'Are you sure?' I asked into her ear, the same question I had asked when she said she would come with us on this journey.

'I guess you were right,' she whispered back. 'I should have gone home.'

She would wait for us for four days. If none of us had returned by then, she would travel back to the tribe and the village and let them know we had failed.

I couldn't imagine Fatima making her way back on her own. I couldn't imagine her coping with staying here, on the fringe, on her own, let alone having to travel. Though I guess I didn't have to imagine it because, if it happened, it would mean I was dead.

How can you truly imagine yourself dead? The only way you are in the world is in this body, with this mind. Without you to look at it, smell it, touch it, hear it, taste it, it can't all continue. I tried not to think of being dead, tried not to think of the fact I had insisted on coming to this place which could get me killed, tried not to toy with the idea of crumpling like Fatima, and pleading not to go.

The harder I tried, the more I thought about it.

Even as we walked slowly up the bitumen road, I glanced back at Fatima, standing with her hands twisted together, with half our bags at her feet. Matthew, Bayat and Oyan had taken theirs, to carry water and food and so we could, hopefully, transport the drug back in them. I imagined myself running down to her, hiding behind her thin shoulders, letting the others continue on.

Thankfully, I didn't do it. Before we had left the village, I had questioned my own strength. Now I knew I did have strength. I could do this. I would do this. It wasn't about me anymore. It was about those I loved. I gripped the bow in my hand and slowly trudged onwards.

The threatening clouds burst open and it began to pour with rain.

Through the veil of water falling from the sky, the outskirts of the city seemed harmless. The road was cracked and broken and the houses which had once lined it were piles of bricks and rotting boards. Touches of green straggled through, lacklustre weeds pushing through the cracks, but everything was mainly black, grey and brown, the rain adding to a sense of dullness. It looked as if a huge wave had surged through, knocking everything over. I suppose this is what had happened, except the wave wasn't made of water. I tried to picture the size of the fireball which could do such a thing. It wouldn't come.

Bayat had said they hadn't seen any of the ferals on this side of the harbour and, for now, I chose to take this as definite proof they didn't live round here. Was 'live' the right word anyway? When they talked of them, the Mountain People made them sound less than human, even if they might have started out that way.

For the moment, I didn't feel afraid, only sad. Maybe my parents had lived in one of these crumbled houses? Maybe that faded red door, splintered in half, had once been the entry to their warm, safe home.

By the time we got to the harbour, I was soaked through. All of us were. Soon I'd start to shiver. This didn't seem like the best way to be entering dangerous territory. How could I possibly shoot an arrow like this? I considered suggesting we go back to Fatima, and wait until the weather turned.

I guess it was my pride that stopped me, since none of the others seemed to be hesitating. They were ploughing on, heads down, wiping the driving tears out of their eyes. Or maybe it was that I also thought it was too late to turn around.

This bridge was one big steel arch. The eight-lane road which once ran over it had collapsed into the waters of the harbour running beneath. I knew our river flowed into this water somewhere further to the east, only I couldn't see any similarity between the beautiful colours of the stream we lived beside, and this vast body of dark liquid. Debris had fallen into it from all sides of the banks, forming islands of trash that had grown over the years with branches and debris from the distant forests.

On the other side was our first real glimpse of what the city might have looked like before The Burning.

Though there was plenty of destruction, there were still skyscrapers standing erect and, as Bayat had said, many large, squat buildings sitting untouched. I didn't feel the same awe as I had at the first bridge. As Bayat had predicted, I'd gotten used to it already, this new landscape of concrete and metal and glass.

'How do we get across?' I asked.

'The steel structure is intact. We just have to climb along it,' Bayat reassured me.

The exposed top of a huge cement pylon stood apart from the unnatural cliff created by the sunken road. We were huddled together a way back from this chasm, though it still seemed too close. It would only take one missed step and you'd plunge into the water and be drowned in all that rubbish. Even as I knew there was no other way, I wished there was. Human beings were so hopeless. We should have developed wings or the ability to climb, like real animals. What I would have given to have padded paws, the assured four-legged movements of the cougar.

The rain stopped, though the sky remained white. We shook ourselves off, my dress still saturated, my skin chilled through.

'This is where we return to, yes?' Bayat didn't have to remind us, though we all looked around, as if we needed to remember the place. Like this might be the last time we had a chance to see our surroundings. Or one another.

I looked at Bayat and he returned my gaze. We didn't say anything. I guess there wasn't anything to say, only sentimental stuff which couldn't be spoken in front of everyone. In my head: *don't die on me*.

'Remember, this is just a scouting mission. We return tomorrow morning with information and go in together against the ferals, if we have to. Whatever you do, don't put yourself in danger.'

We murmured our assurances.

Matthew and I made our way to the far-left side of the bridge, where the steel struts jutted over the precipice. The inner horizontal girder was wide enough for us to walk sideways and we began to shuffle along, gripping the crosspieces as we went. The other four took the right-hand side of the bridge because it would take them closer to their designated search areas.

As soon as Bayat, Titus, Emmaline and Oyan were out of sight, when their bodies became just blurred movements in the distance, I forced myself to forget about them.

It wasn't hard. Once we were past the relative shelter of the towering pylon, the wind hit full force, like having someone slapping at your back, smack after smack after smack, cutting into cold skin. Worse still, sprays of water sporadically swirled up from the harbour, hitting me in the face. I couldn't close my eyes to avoid it and, soon, I had a foul taste in my mouth from where the drips had found their way to my tongue.

'How are you doing?' Matthew shouted back to me. He'd taken the lead. Thankfully, we were almost at the other side.

'I'm having the time of my life!' I yelled, wondering if my sarcasm would be lost in the gale.

'Really?' He stopped moving and looked intently back at me. *By the rivers*, he didn't get me sometimes ...

'Just keep going!'

I made the mistake of looking down. Directly below was a raised island of what seemed to be thin strips of pale concrete. I tried to fight off the vertigo that came from finally understanding how high we were, hearing the howling squalls around me, and slowly realised it was a huge pile of rabrat bones. I held my breath, determined not to suck in any of the air above this grave, and started shuffling along again.

Bones. At least, we hadn't seen any sign of human ... remains ... in our walk through the city. It'd been as if no people ever lived there. But the mass grave of animal remains spoke of occupation, of creatures who needed sustenance … I decided not to mention it to Matthew. There was already too much to be afraid of.

15

Matthew and I made it to the other side. I looked to where the others were also climbing over the metal, back onto the concrete road. All four were there. Bayat gave a small wave before he and Titus ran down the road, heading south. Oyan and Emmaline didn't acknowledge us and disappeared over the lip of the bridge embankment, towards the west. I gave Matthew a tiny smile and hurried towards a small road leading off to the left, into the city's eastern district. This time, I would be leading.

Amongst buildings which were still together, even if their windows were empty and parts of their walls crumbling, I finally got a taste of what it might have been like to live in the city. Although the day was dull,

I knew it must have been almost always cold, the sun not really able to penetrate through these masses of dark material. Yet, if the harbour had once been like our river water, it would've sparkled beautifully, making up for these shadows. I tried to picture the many, many, many swarming these streets but, with only the sound of lapping waves and the ever-present wind, it felt quieter than our village. A space so large and empty. Despite the bones, I didn't feel any great sense of foreboding. I was convinced we were alone. No human could possibly exist in this place of ruins. And the creatures? I still couldn't picture them, so I chose not to imagine them here.

We made our way towards the tallest edifice. Made of stone and almost completely without damage, it was set back from the harbour's edge, up a series of low steps. Six rows of windows ran up along its rectangular front, with a pointy structure in its centre. I couldn't see any letters to indicate what the place was. It did remind me of old photos of hospitals, small square panes lined along its front like dead eyes. They would have once had glass in them.

'Did you see that?' Matthew paused, one foot on the step next to me.

'See what?'

'I thought I saw something move, in one of the windows, near the top.'

I stopped too, looking up to where Matthew had indicated. I couldn't see anything.

'Are you sure?' I asked.

'No.'

My heart beat quickened, my confidence evaporated.

'Should we go in there?' I didn't want to chance it. Then again, this might be the right place. We needed to check.

'Bayat said not to risk anything, Pan. That if there was even the possibility of encountering ...'

This was definitely the first time I'd ever heard Matthew quoting Bayat. I knew he was right. Like Bayat had said, this was only supposed to be a preliminary scout. No heroics. Determine what might be a possible place for the drugs and return to the meeting point.

If we didn't go in, though, we couldn't rule this building out.

'We need to check if it's a hospital or not, Matthew. Otherwise, someone else will have to do it.'

Matthew nodded. He glanced up at the window again and so did I. There still wasn't anything there. Maybe he'd just imagined it.

As we climbed the final set of stairs, I reached over my shoulder for an arrow and notched it into my bow. Beside me, Matthew unsheathed his knife.

The huge wooden doors which had once stood in the entrance lay flat on the ground, as if pushed by a giant, frames rotted and decayed. The floor on which they lay was like nothing I'd ever seen before: under a layer of dust there was something light pink and when I reached down and wiped the greyness away I saw it was like river stone, except polished smooth. Ahead were gigantic rooms with this same floor, one leading on to the next, with only parts of walls to separate them. We walked slowly into the first of them, cautiously checking for any signs of inhabitation. There wasn't any furniture, no rusting beds or chairs, as if no one had ever lived or done anything here. I knew this wasn't the right kind of place. I lowered my bow in disappointment.

I found Matthew gazing at something on the wall and as he used the sleeve of his shirt to rub at the dirt on the surface of the thing, I realised all the walls were covered with these same kinds of objects.

'It's an art gallery,' Matthew said, too loudly, for it seemed to echo everywhere.

I walked to the opposite wall. There was a square

piece of art hanging on it and I blew hard at it, sending a shower of dust over myself. I started coughing, making even more noise. For the moment, though, I was too amazed by the colours I'd revealed. A picture of a deep blue sky above rusted red sand, with bright purple mountains in the distance. All faded. Still, the deepest hues I'd ever seen created. The centre of the picture had rotted. A figure might have stood there once, looking towards, or away, from the mountains.

'It's …'

Matthew's art was behind glass, its paper curling at the corners. It showed the inside of a grey box, full of smoky cloud, with four horizontal lines of colour at its end: orange, green, blue and red, painted to look like they were lit from within. I felt a weird kind of longing, I wanted to reach into it, to be inside it.

How had the people who had made these things let the civilised world end? How had this beauty not been enough to preserve them? I thought again of my mother and had a glimpse as to why she was always sad. And why she hadn't wanted to look back. There was so much I couldn't appreciate or understand but here, in front of these works of art, I could almost get it.

Then we heard the clicking sound.

If I had tried to imagine what the creatures looked like, what the ferals were going to be, it wasn't anything like the female face which now glared at us around the corner of the wall. Her hair was short and white, matted onto her head, and her skin was a weird, mottled orange. She stared, her eyes also orange, with thin black vertical lines in their centres.

She slinked around the corner, her short, dirty dress showing her legs to be the same strange colour. Other than the eyes and the hue of her skin, she looked just like all the other human beings I'd ever seen in my life which, I admit, isn't that many. She seemed to be walking normally, only a bit slowly, cautiously padding towards us.

I'd expected some kind of clear deformity, something to make them distinctly not-like-us. This was a human being changed, yes, but still … human?

I had raised my bow instinctively, ready to fire at a hideous thing. Now I was frozen, wondering how I could possibly hurt her. She only looked a couple of notches older than my mother.

Then she snarled, her mouth dropping open as

she twisted her head to the side, revealing rows of teeth sharpened into points and with two long fangs. My stomach flipped. With a growl, she continued slowly creeping towards us and I realised the clicking sound was her toenails, transformed into razor-like talons, tapping against the stone. I was transfixed by her hands, fingernails also stretched and sharp.

'Shoot it!' Matthew yelled.

I should have let the arrow fly. I should have aimed at her heart. Instead, I stood there stupidly. Was she something less – or more – than human?

Suddenly, she pounced across the space, on all fours, covering an amazing distance to throw herself onto Matthew. He fell backwards, into the artwork. The glass cracked against his skull and the two bodies crashed to the floor.

The creature let out another cry. This time, one of pain. Matthew's knife was sticking out of her side. She was still thrashing on top of him, Matthew using his other hand to hold her back, pushing at her neck. She was trying to bite him.

I threw down my bow and arrow and pulled out my knife. I heard Bayat's taunting words in my head: *Why are you waiting? Will the feral wait until you're good and ready?*

Why was I waiting?

She is not human, I told myself, she is not human, she is not human.

I sprinted to them and thrust the knife into the centre of the creature's back, feeling the blade push through skin and muscle. I let go of the handle, staggering away.

The creature screamed and rolled off Matthew, onto the side where the other knife protruded, driving it deeper into herself. She twitched and convulsed on the cold stone, wiggled for a moment longer and stopped moving altogether.

I ran from her into a corner and threw up. My vomit tasted of berries. I stayed leaning over, smelling the pile of sick. I was panting. It felt like I couldn't get enough air into me. I had killed her. *By the rivers*, I had killed her.

'Pan? Pan?'

Matthew was calling for me from beside her dead body. He hadn't managed to get up. As I peered over at him – he seemed to be about a thousand worlds away – I saw there was blood on his face, streaming into his eye.

'Pan! Help me! Did it bite me? Did it get in?'

The panic in his voice brought me back to myself. I could breathe normally again.

I ran to Matthew and helped him sit up.

'It's only my blood isn't it? Isn't it?'

I didn't know why he was so spooked but I checked the wound. It was only his blood trailing down his face.

'*Thank the rivers ...*'

'What are you so worried about? She's dead.'

'It was trying to bite me, Pan. Don't you remember Rama's lessons about viruses? Transmission by bodily fluids?'

'So?'

'So, no one knows where these ferals came from. But don't you see how they are some kind of hybrid ...'

I tried to piece it together. The science that had been developed to create the goateeps and the rabrats ...

'Someone *made* these ... creatures?' I couldn't bring myself to use the word 'feral', for the moment, it seemed too cruel to speak it out loud.

'I think so. And, maybe, the condition can be passed on ... in saliva or blood.'

We both looked at the body of the feral. In death, her eyes and mouth closed, she'd lost the savage mask of her transformation and, if not for the colour of her skin and the shape of her nails, she could've just been an ordinary woman. Yes, if not for those markers. I almost laughed at the absurdity of me trying to make her the same as us.

'It's a good thing there was only one of them,' Matthew spoke quietly. 'We didn't do that well.'

'No, I didn't exactly do Bayat proud.' As soon as the words came out of my mouth, I knew they were the wrong ones.

'And, of course, you mustn't disappoint Bayat.'

At least I knew Matthew wasn't seriously hurt, his jealousy was definitely intact.

'We should get out of here, Matthew.'

'I can't see all that well.'

'Here.'

I leant over and ripped some cloth off the creature's dress. It was thread-bare but, when I scrunched it into a ball and poured some water onto it, I could wash Matthew's eye well enough.

I cleaned the wound as well. A chunk of glass must have cut through the top of his forehead, just where the skin met the hairline, though it was more bloody than deep. He'd been lucky.

'That's me,' he said, when I told him this. 'Lucky Matthew.'

I'd never known him to be so sarcastic.

'I don't understand how Bayat wouldn't have picked up on the transmission process.' Matthew seemed determined to be critical of him and I couldn't let it pass.

'If he hadn't learnt about such things, why would he?'

'No, he was too busy killing things to actually use his brain.'

'Matthew, what did *we* just do?'

I couldn't actually bring myself to look at the body of the woman again. The artwork I'd been examining before the attack still sat on the wall opposite us, the gaping hole where a figure had once stood, like the hole I'd just created by taking a life.

'We killed in self-defence,' Matthew insisted.

'Bayat would have done the same.'

'Not from what I've heard.'

'What are you talking about?'

From above our heads, a crashing sound.

'There's more of them,' Matthew whispered, fear in his voice.

'We have to go.'

We jumped up. Without thinking, I pulled the knife from the creature's back. Matthew retrieved his knife as well, still holding the rag to his head wound. I ran to collect my bow and the discarded arrow. The two of us sprinted along the pink stone floor and out into the open. On the steps we stopped to look back. There, at the windows of the fifth level, were the faces of the ferals.

They were all similar to the woman we'd seen: matted hair and horrible coloured skin. Men and women, all showing their chiselled teeth and fangs, growling in rage at us through the glass. I counted fifteen, my heart pounding, knowing there was no way we could fight them off. We would have to run and hide.

The faces disappeared; they were coming for us.

Suddenly, standing in the doorway we had just passed through was the woman. The same woman we had stuck two knives into.

She was not dead.

Swiftly, I notched the arrow into my bow and aimed it at her. We were at the bottom of the steps and she was a perfect target, standing high on the broken doors, framed by the light behind her. She did not move, only snarled at me again and, for a moment, I thought I saw something flash in her face.

I closed my eyes and imagined Bayat beside me, murmuring. *Set her free.*

I opened my eyes and released the bow. The arrow shot straight and up, directly into her heart. Her body flew backwards, slamming into the splintered ground.

We could hear the baying of the other creatures, getting closer.

We fled. We had a head start. That was about our only advantage. We had to make the most of it.

'How did that thing come alive again?' Matthew asked as we ran. 'How could it have survived our knives?'

'Bayat told us to aim for the heart.'

'And he didn't want to mention that, otherwise, they don't stay dead?'

I didn't want to think about this. This wasn't the time to be arguing about the finer points of Bayat's training.

16

We ran up a hill, along a road lined with dead trees, their gnarled branches like skeletons waving in the wind. At the top, we had to stop to catch our breath. To the left, another road to the harbour, a field of brown grass hugging the pavement. To the right, a collection of completely demolished buildings, huge piles of collapsed concrete. I didn't dare to glance behind me and I knew I didn't want us to get caught against the water. I might have been able to swim to the other side, but I didn't think Matthew was strong enough, not with his wound. I began to run towards the south, vaguely hoping this might bring us closer to Bayat and Titus. It was a long shot.

'Wouldn't we be better off heading towards the harbour?' Matthew yelled after me. I stopped and turned back to him. Inadvertently, I gazed down the hill, expecting to see the creatures running towards us, the horde about to attack. There was nothing. No one.

'Where are they?'

Matthew looked too.

'But they were coming after us ...'

I remembered the pile of bones I had seen under the bridge and thought of the creature I had shot. Her body in the doorway. Maybe they didn't just eat rabrats? I gagged.

'What is it?' Matthew asked.

'Maybe they've been ... distracted.'

'By what?'

'The ... the creature ... I shot. Maybe they ... eat each other?'

Matthew went even whiter than normal, if that was possible, and looked like he was going to throw up too.

'We have to make the most of it.' I was trying to be practical, trying to block out the image of those things ... 'I think we can circle back to the bridge this way.'

'Wouldn't it be easier to swim?'

'I'm not going in that water.'

I had tried to use Matthew as an excuse. It wasn't that. I couldn't stand the idea of it, of going near the bones.

Matthew opened his mouth, as if to argue. Then, thankfully, he shut it again and nodded.

'Okay, let's go.'

We didn't run at full speed, we were already too tired, and it seemed foolish to pelt through streets which might hold new dangers. We jogged, my bow and arrow at the ready, Matthew's knife in his hand, taking the precautions we should have when we first entered the city. I couldn't really believe I'd been so casual before, as if I hadn't believed in the creatures, as if I'd considered them to be something from a dream I wasn't going to have. Now I was in the nightmare. I suspected the face of the feral I'd shot would never leave my head, particularly her expression just before the arrow flew. Could it really have been *relief*? Could those things even feel emotion anymore?

We made our way along an open avenue. Rain drizzled down again and I couldn't tell if the shaking of my body was from the cold or the wet or the terror. Maybe all three. I wanted so much to be back in my village, to be doing all the boring things I'd complained about, to be safe inside its boundaries again, the net Theodore had cast around us. Even though I knew it was fake now, it had all been an illusion, it would be nice to go back to it for a while, to not know what was out here. Impossible, of course. Now I knew, there was no going back. No forgetting the creatures and their savage faces ...

'Let's head down here.' Matthew was leading again. He veered to the right, taking another open plaza which seemed to be heading back downhill, parallel but farther away from the art gallery. There were collapsed holes sporadically located along the way, steps that seemed to be leading underground. What was below us? There had been lessons about metal vehicles which travelled both through and above the surface. I couldn't remember what they were called. Planes? Or was it trains?

In the distance the sound of a strangled scream. Matthew and I stopped. The silence resumed.

'Did that sound like Emmaline to you?' Matthew asked.

I shrugged. I didn't want to think of any of us making such a noise. Useless to try and guess where it'd come from, the wind distorted direction too much. The smell of the harbour blew into our noses.

A tall, white building, almost completely intact,

stood in front of us. I followed its vertical height – there were, at least, thirty levels – amazed at how it had withstood the wars and spotted a strange symbol on the outside, at the top.

'What is that?'

Matthew looked hard too and, almost at the same time, we gasped with our recognition.

It was the outline of a great cat. Not quite a cougar, its middle was too wide, but a similar shape, thin white tubes marking its body and head. It was stalking, front paw and back foot lifted to convey movement. Once, I understood, this picture would have been lit up from the inside, like the colours in the painting we'd seen, along with the word written beside it.

I didn't know the word, my limited reading had always been about recognising words, not sounding them out. Matthew had always done better.

'What does it say, Matthew?'

He paused for a second, mouthing the letters one by one.

'K.A.P.L.A.N.'

'Which is …?'

'Kaplan.'

This time, only I gasped.

It took some convincing to make Matthew agree to go into the white building.

'So, you heard the word Kaplan in your vision, Pan. Why does that make it significant?'

'How can it not be significant? Why would she have whispered it to me otherwise?'

'*She?* The cat was an *it* and, in case you haven't noticed, animals can't talk.'

I so wished I was with Bayat. He was a reader. He would've believed me, he would've understood how not everything is explicable or reasonable or ... safe.

'I'm going into that place, Matthew, whether you come with me or not.'

I had already started towards the entrance, jumping over the shattered glass of the floor-to-ceiling windows. Directly in front of me was a large white slab of stone and, behind it, a row of metal doors.

'Pan, just wait for a moment.'

I paused to let him come up beside me.

'I know you think your time after the cougar attack was something ... special.'

I didn't look at him. I wondered how to make one

of these metal doors open. None of them seemed to have a way in.

'But I've read about these kind of things. Medical people used to call it going into shock, like Emmaline did after finding Theodore ill. Your trauma was just as big, having the cat attack you. Anything you saw, or heard, was just from your own imagination.'

Matthew was so supremely good at talking about things I didn't want to talk about. What was it about him that thought I needed to be brought down to earth, reminded of my insecurities? How could he not see I was struggling to make sense of everything? Why did he always have to act as if he had all the answers?

I didn't say anything.

At the far corner of the ground floor, I spotted an open wooden door. I approached it cautiously, remembering our failing at the art gallery.

Matthew followed behind me, silent at last.

The stairwell was wide with red coloured metal steps, spotted with rust holes. Still, they held our weight as we climbed, floor after floor. I didn't know what I was looking for exactly, what sign I expected to tell me when to enter the building. Only I wanted to keep going. Although I was panting, I didn't feel as exhausted as I would have before the training, my legs strained but still strong. All the running had paid off. I smiled, thinking of Bayat's muscled back ahead of me, the incentive it gave me to keep moving. I felt the warmth which always flowed into me when I thought of him.

'Here.'

We had reached the top of the building. I peered down through the square hole inside the stairs, back down to the distant bottom, knowing this was the highest building I had ever been in, so far from the ground.

I pulled open the metal door and stepped into a world of whiteness. A long corridor with walls and ceiling and columns and floors like a shimmering frost. Unlike the art gallery, it had not accumulated a layer of dust, as if someone – or something – had been cleaning it regularly. It was hard to imagine the ferals as housekeepers.

Lined along the corridor were six doors, placed at regular intervals, each with a circular, glass window. None of these were broken and when I looked through the first of these holes, I realised the outer windows were not smashed either. We couldn't hear the wind anymore. Just quietness. Definitely creepy.

'What is this place?' Matthew whispered.

I knew it wasn't a hospital. We opened the first door and realised each one of the doors led to this same space. Another field of white: long stone benches dotted like broken rectangles running down the middle of the room and there was a bank of empty metal shelves on the wall opposite the giant windows. Again, it was all clean. Spotless.

The only jarring note was a huge metal circle – a wheel – on a steel door embedded into the facing wall, layered in grime.

I had no words for what this place might have been, couldn't picture what might have happened here. Something had led me here and I wasn't going to let Matthew's doubts kick in, not yet.

Through the windows we could see the city spread out below, the ravaged mess and the pockets of surviving land. We were four or five blocks away from the art gallery and the harbour. From this height, it seemed only a few footsteps. The sky had turned a dirty pale grey.

'Let's try the door,' I said.

We stood in front of the giant wheel. I figured you would spin it to allow the door to open.

'Pan, there might be a reason no one's touched that door.'

'Come on, Matthew, what could be in there that's worse than what's out here?'

I felt reckless.

I was the legend: Pandora, letting loose horror and destruction. The city had got to me. This bleak wasteland. Nothing could be more awful.

'Do not touch that!'

We spun around. An old man stood in one of the doorways, his shoulders back, glaring at us in the gloom. Without thinking, I raised my bow and arrow and aimed it at his heart. The old man didn't flinch.

'I'm quite human.'

Was I being duped again? Would he show his pointed teeth and rush towards me? My bow quivered. I didn't want to let Matthew down again.

'He's not one of them, Pan.' Matthew spoke quietly, knowing I was on edge. 'You can put it down.'

I lowered the bow. I still couldn't bring myself to un-notch the arrow.

The old man strode into the room and I saw he was not that old. Although he had long grey hair pulled back into a ponytail, he moved easily enough, his body thin and relatively healthy looking. He wore a long grey cloak made out of what looked like rabrat skins and wrapped around his neck was a strange bulky fur scarf. In his hand he carried a piece of skin covered in dust. He stood in front of the giant wheeled door.

'What are you doing here, young ones?'

The question sounded abrupt and rude. I didn't want to answer him straight away. I didn't know if we could trust him.

'Do you live here? Alone?' I asked.

There must have been others. He could not have lived in the city, with the creatures, on his own.

'I am a guardian.'

He didn't say anything more. Moving past, he suddenly started wiping at the window with his dusty rag, as if he'd forgotten us.

'A guardian of what?'

He stopped dusting and turned to smile at us.

'You think the worst has come, young ones? There are worse things behind that door. I keep them safe.'

'How have you survived?'

He looked out the window, although it wasn't clear if he was seeing anything before him.

'There are ways.'

He began to clean again, now bending to rub at a spot of dirt on the floor, which either Matthew or I were responsible for.

'What is your name?' This was the first time Matthew spoke. He had been staring at the man, his expression almost as horrified as when he saw the creatures. I was embarrassed by the fact I hadn't even thought to ask what the man's name was.

He didn't answer, moving to the bench tops and continuing with his task.

'You should go now. They will come for you.'

'The ferals?' Matthew asked.

Again, the old man stopped. This time, he turned back towards me.

'You should remember they were once just like you.'

I thought of the flash of emotion I'd seen in the woman I'd shot, but still I couldn't believe he wanted us to feel sorry for them.

'They tried to kill us!'

'Did they?' he asked. 'Or, maybe, they were just trying to … expand. They want you to join them. I would have done so, long ago, if I didn't have another duty.'

Matthew moved closer to me, putting his hand on my shoulder.

'He's totally mad,' he whispered in my ear.

Maybe Matthew was right, but I couldn't shake the feeling the man, like he had claimed of the creatures, was connected to me.

'How haven't you been … made … to join them?' I asked.

'I have my ways.'

I realised we were wasting time. Either he could help us, or not.

'We need to find medicine,' I explained. 'In our village, a long way from here, my father and many others are very sick. My mother told me to find a drug which would save them. We were supposed to find a hospital but we ended up here ...'

The man's rag kept moving. Had he even heard me?

'There's nothing here for us, Pan. It's just another dead end. Come on,' Matthew urged, heading for the doorway, 'we have to get back to the bridge.'

It was hopeless. Who wouldn't go crazy living alone in this empty building? Who wouldn't start to believe you were guarding the world from more horror? There was probably nothing behind the door, just this old man's nightmares. I would have to leave him to it. But I tried one last time.

'The drug is called ... ZarVex.'

He looked up and there was a sparkle of recognition.

'There is none of that left here.' For the first time, the man sounded defensive.

Matthew stopped. 'So, there was some here? Before?' he asked.

The man had stopped cleaning.

'No ... I mean, yes, long ago.'

I knew he was lying.

'Where is it?' I spoke quietly. Only as I said it did I realise I was still holding my bow and arrow. An unspoken threat.

<h1 style="text-align:center">17</h1>

My heart raced like crazy as we clambered down one flight of stairs. The floor below was the exact replica of the one we had just left, except layered in dirt and dust. Cobwebs hung from the ceiling and rabrat droppings littered the ground. In the same position as the vaulted door we had seen closed on the level above, the same thick steel door stood open. Inside, in a room without windows, there were shelves upon shelves lined with small square boxes.

I picked up one of the boxes and opened the lid carefully. In a spongy material lay six glass vials with the letter 'Z' engraved on them, exactly as my mother had described them.

'This is it,' Matthew said, wonder in his voice. 'We found it.'

But as we examined the boxes more closely, we realised most of them were empty. There weren't enough untouched, only about ten boxes. Enough for our village and enough for Bayat's tribe, if no one else had got sick since we left. We couldn't think about that now. We carefully filled Matthew's bag, lying the boxes on top of one another. In a drawer in the room outside I found the needles we'd need to administer the clear liquid.

Matthew and I grinned stupidly, hardly able to believe our success. Our luck. Or was it luck? Something had brought me here and I thought, again, of the vision that had led us here.

I glanced up from stuffing the needles into the bag and saw a face at the round window. My elation mistook it for the old man, following us. Then came the growl. It was not the old man.

'They're here!' I screamed, bundling the bag into my arms and running for the end door, Matthew behind me.

At the far end of the corridor, in front of the first of the six entrances, was a group of ferals. They swivelled, as one, in our direction. Though they were all orange-skinned, I could still distinguish the three females from the four males. They were not the same group as the one from the art gallery. A tribe of seven, with the one I had just seen at the window, a streak of black showing on his white, matted head, seeming to be their leader. He snarled, as if to signal, and they began creeping towards us. I realised I had left my bow and arrow behind.

Our only escape was down the steps, but the creatures had just come up them and were in between us and the stairwell. I pushed Matthew back into the room. If we could weave our way past the doors inside here and get behind them …

'Take the bag.' I shoved it at Matthew. I figured the vials were in their protected material, any rough treatment would have to be covered by this. I knew we couldn't afford to lose any, but there wasn't anything else to do.

I retrieved my bow and arrow, thinking about what had happened last time. Perhaps all I needed to do was kill one of them and this would distract the rest. The idea made me queasy. But if it was a question of survival …

I knew I'd prefer to try to outrun them again. Get back to the bridge. Get back to the others.

You should remember they were once just like you.

At each one of the six windows, at each one of the doors, appeared the hideous face of one of my supposed kin. No chance of escape now.

I ducked behind one of the benches, ready for

the first of them to come through the door, to let my arrow fly.

'Get in here!' Matthew shouted, sprinting into the windowless room where we'd just got the drug. *By the rivers*, what was he doing?

'Pan!' He was pulling the huge steel door closed. 'Come on!'

Before I could think, I followed him in, grabbing the long handle and closing out the light. In the darkness, I heard Matthew spin the wheel lock. The door sealed.

I guess Matthew thought it was a good idea at the time. Right now he's complaining about his bleeding wound – he managed to bang his head again while stumbling around in the dark – and I am trying to be sympathetic.

The creatures are on the other side of the door. I have no idea how we are going to get out without being swamped by them or if they are capable of figuring out how to get in here. I don't think we are going to survive and I finally understand what Matthew was trying to tell me before. My vision wasn't any kind of premonition. It was stupid to bring us into this building, even if we have found the ZarVex. I should have listened. We should have waited to come back with the others. With Bayat.

I'm going to die – or, maybe worse, get turned into a feral – and my mother and father will die, without ever seeing me again. They will know I've failed and they will think of me that way at their end: the daughter who tried, but who ultimately let them down.

LETTERS

3

Pandora,

These last few days have been the hardest of my life. I was certain your father was going to die. He fell into a burning fever. We hadn't seen this in the others. Most of the time they're relatively tranquil and we are more concerned about them wasting away because they eat so little, even while they are constantly thirsty. So, your father's condition was unusual, and frightening. There was nothing to be done, of course. All our hopes still rest with you and your friends.

I could only try to keep Hector comfortable. I reassured him when he called for you how you'd be coming soon. I know you will find it hard to understand how I could lie to him but he needed it, Pan. To believe you were within reach. He was screaming for you. Convinced you were in mortal danger. I can only cling to the hope this was all a result of his delirium and nothing more, no kind of sign. Yes, I know your father hates superstition but, like you, I can't help it.

After two days the fever, miraculously, broke. Writing to you now is the first time I have left his side because he is sleeping soundly and I'm only doing so because Rama insisted I come here to get some rest. She doesn't know I've kept some paper to continue my story for you. She doesn't understand I can't possibly sleep without speaking to you, without continuing my explanation. The thought of losing your father reminded me again of how much I've kept back from you. How much more devastated you will be if you lose him, rather than me.

No, I don't blame you for loving him more. Who wouldn't? Maybe you will understand me better if you know what we went through, if you can try to comprehend the time before The Burning. I know you asked me many times and I'm sorry now for my stubbornness in not talking to you about it. Then again, maybe this is the best way for you to know the story, especially if we're no longer here to tell you.

After Louise's death, the days seemed even slower

because everyone moved more cautiously. We didn't even dare to bring out the live virus of H1T3. Ivan became almost obsessive about guarding the vault in which the samples were stored. Although I didn't have much sympathy for him at the time, I look back now and know he was racked with guilt.

It was in this time – between the disaster and Hector's release – we realised the potential of the drug, ZarVex. As I said, we were able to witness its outstanding ability to cure.

Pan, perhaps you will have worked out by now how illnesses come from all sorts of sources, how the root-juice consumed on the day of the Blossoming was the cause of our current epidemic. I have not had time to investigate but I am willing to bet the secret site of the roots we use to make the drink has been contaminated. I have no idea how, since we've been living here for so long without anything like this happening before. When this is over – however it all ends up – we, or you, will have to find out. The difference in response to the disease has, I believe, a link to different natural levels of resistance. They are all doomed nonetheless, if you don't bring back the drug. Still, I mustn't think about that now.

When Hector was released from quarantine, he returned to the apartment he lived in, on the same floor as Ivan and I. Even though I had long since stopped loving Ivan, I didn't like the deception of those final weeks. Hector and I had to continue to work in the lab, pretending to have no feelings, whilst desperately wanting to be near each other. Ivan's new habit of often sleeping in his office gave us a chance, at night, to meet and plan our escape.

We had decided to leave Melney as soon as we could. I wasn't prescient. Even though I had my concerns about where things were heading, it was more Hector's urging than anything. He had heard rumours, listened to talk of small settlements deliberately being established 'outside', beyond the boundaries of the city. Yes, we had our boundaries back then, too. And there were more than just rules and conventions keeping them in place. I have heard you grumbling, Pan, about the way in which the village tries to 'keep everyone in'. At the risk of sounding like a know-it-all adult, you really have no idea.

I didn't think it through. I was willing to do anything and everything for Hector and, although a small part of me niggled – the tiny part which knew I should go out and try to help what was left of humanity – I was too selfish to really listen to that voice. I wanted to be away from Ivan and my parents. I wanted a fresh start, as if we could walk into the wilderness, forget the past and begin all over again.

We left at night. The fifty-foot steel fence which surrounded our 'community' was easy enough to cut through, it had always been more of a symbol than a real deterrent. The actual security was the Officers, with hand-guns and vicious dogs, who patrolled 24/7, though money could keep them away from a certain section for a certain amount of time. Easier still, because we were breaking out, not in.

Omar and Petty were waiting for us on the other side. I still remember how the edge of the steel fence caught on the strap of my backpack, making me cry out. I thought someone was grabbing me.

'A jumpy one, isn't she?' These were Petty's first words, leaning against the small green car they had packed up with all their stuff, smoking a cigarette, her thin, wiry body evident in a mini-skirt, knee-high boots and tank top. Having spent most of my life trying to cover up my body, I was hit with a mix of admiration and envy. Her long black hair flowed freely over her shoulders.

Petty wasn't looking at me, though, she was addressing Hector. His face clouded for a moment before he smiled. 'She's fine.'

Hector, Petty and Omar had grown up together, in places I had never set foot. She thought I was a spoiled princess.

'It's wonderful to finally meet you,' Omar said and came to take my hand in-between his own. His kind eyes were such a relief. 'Hector has spoken about you for a long time.'

I blushed, although they were probably unable to see it in the weak light of the street lamps, so many of them were smashed or broken.

I breathed in the strange new air. It tasted of burnt meat. For so many years, I had travelled from my home to the lab via the underground Bullet – a highly expensive mode of transport available to the privileged few – and only ever took in unconditioned air on the tiny balcony of our apartment. Even then, Ivan had warned me not to do this often, worried about snipers or toxic gas attacks.

I shivered and Hector put his arms around me. I leant back into his chest, feeling safe, and tried not to worry how we would negotiate these dark streets and alleys, how we would avoid gangs who apparently ambushed and kidnapped any 'rich-bitch', how I would possibly survive without the protection of my parents or Ivan.

Petty threw down the butt of her cigarette and opened the back-passenger door.

'Your carriage awaits,' she said sarcastically.

When I remember that night it has the quality of a dream: the car filled with Petty's cigarette smoke; my own fearful face in the dark glass of the car window; fires burning in the shanty towns we passed. We moved silently – the car ran on electric batteries – and there were only a few other vehicles on the road. I compared it to the trips I had taken as a child, before the oil ran out, the splutter and chug of petrol engines, surrounded by traffic, hundreds of other metal beasts going in all directions. How would you have felt, Pan? You, who have never moved except through the volition of your own feet?

What surprised me most was the lack of people. In the news feeds we were constantly shown riots: masses of angry, vicious poor who always seemed to need submission by brutal force. As we passed through the areas which were supposed to be hotspots, all I saw were broken down houses, half-completed apartment buildings, chunks of land with nothing on them except rubbish and piles of rusted girders. There was only a scattering of inhabitants: a group of teenagers, what you know as those who have Blossomed, throwing a basketball around a cracked piece of bitumen; an old man lit by one functioning street lamp, gaping down into an empty gutter, his head jerking up to follow our passing; a young woman, sprinting along the pavement, her face full of terror, before veering into an alley, into the darkness. Small, strange glimpses of a world I no longer knew.

Only as we got closer to the centre did I begin to recognise places: the formidable sandstone of the Modern Art Gallery, still standing thanks to one member of the ruling group who liked paintings; the hollowed-out library, with no such luck, its blackened walls a testimony to the new ignorance and, of course, the lab or, as I still couldn't quite bring myself to call it, the Kaplan building.

There it was, as we turned off the main avenue towards the bridge, flashing in orange and white neon, the sign of the tiger stalking across the top of our white edifice, an animal I had never seen in the flesh, since it was extinct by the time I was born. I remember Hector squeezing my hand tightly as we drove past it. I kept my face turned away from his so he couldn't see me crying. I wouldn't have been able to explain what was making me weep – I had no regrets, no desire to return to that place – only I didn't quite know what I was getting myself into, and the tears came from feeling weak. I looked up at the building. Was Ivan awake or asleep? What would he dream of when he knew I had left him?

Crossing the bridge, the dark blue waters of the harbour spread out on either side of us, I wiped my eyes and squared my shoulders. I vowed not to cry again. Not to let Petty have another excuse to look at me in the rear vision mirror with contempt. Not to embarrass Hector again. Though I thought it was a good idea at the time – to make myself hard and invulnerable – I'm not sure you will be pleased to know it is a promise I have kept all these years.

You have never seen me cry, Pan, and I know you think I'm cold because of it. This is why I have to write and explain. For you to see what it is that has made me the way I am. Children always think their parents came into the world fully formed. You have to understand I have been made, just as you are being made, with every decision you take, with every choice you make.

Rama has just caught me writing and insists I finish off and have some rest. I have to admit I am very tired and, as she has pointed out, it will mean more work for everyone if I get too run down to do my duties. I am sorry to leave you here, Pan. Take care, my brave daughter, and I will endeavour to tell you the rest of my story when I am rested.

Your loving mother,

Zaana

Part Four

18

'Why did you bring us in here?' I ask and Matthew shakes his head.

'I don't know. I just didn't think.'

I should have known how ridiculously unprepared we were. All my arrogance about us being able to do anything. The River People aren't fighters or strategists or heroes. We have lived in a tiny village all our lives. How can we be expected to deal with this? I don't feel angry with Matthew. I could've made the same mistake. I only wish I'd gone with my instincts, and started shooting.

'I can't die,' I say.

We are huddled together against the furthest wall from the door. The darkness is no longer total, my eyes have adjusted enough to make out the faint lines of Matthew and the shelves. I am finding it difficult to breathe but I think this is just my imagination.

Matthew says we should be able to survive a few hours in this airless space.

We can hear that the creatures are still on the other side of the door. They keep growling and snarling. I wonder if they are calling out to more of them and if we open it, they'll overrun us before I've had time to re-string my bow. Perhaps they'll get bored and stumble away. Do they have the capacity for boredom? And are we going to suffocate to death beforehand?

'I can't die,' I repeat.

'Any particular reason?' Matthew's voice is weak and low. I am glad to hear it, though, to confirm he's still with me. He hasn't spoken for a while.

'My parents will be very disappointed in me.'

Matthew snorts.

'*That's* your biggest reason for living?'

I remember kissing Bayat for the first time. I close my eyes and feel the same rush as I did then.

When I open my eyes, Matthew's shadow is looming above mine. He is breathing heavily.

'Are you sure there are no other reasons for wanting to live?'

I know he wants me to give him some kind of sign. He won't try anything without absolute assurance I won't reject him. In the darkness, I close my eyes again. I can't think of what to say. I don't know what it is I want right now.

I sense him moving and feel his lips gently touch mine. It's nothing like Bayat's kiss. It is tentative and afraid, but I'm not revolted by it. It is just different. I open my mouth and let his tongue come in. I feel the weight of his body move onto mine. I feel his hardness.

I'm totally amazed he could be feeling this way, in this situation. Creatures baying for our blood at the door and he wants to do *it*?

I pull my head back, breaking off the slow kiss.

'I don't think this is the right time, Matthew.'

'We might die in the next few hours,' he says. 'This is definitely the right time.'

They're almost exactly the same words I'd tried to convince Bayat with and, with them, our 'almost' night comes back to me. The way in which Bayat paused to let me consider, his respect of Matthew as my Chosen, the beautiful way we stood together, under the moon.

I push Matthew off me and stand up. Stupidly, I feel guiltier for having betrayed Bayat in kissing Matthew, rather than the other way around.

'I can't die,' I say, for the third time and I suddenly know we need a plan of escape. No one is coming for us. There isn't going to be any last-minute rescue. We have to get out of this room. We have to get back across the bridge and deliver ZarVex to our village and Bayat's tribe. We have to live.

We push three of the metal shelves onto their sides, to form a barrier which almost takes up the length of the room. I hate to hear these unknown medicines break and burst upon the ground, but we don't have the ability to do it more carefully in the almost-blackness. The vertical shelves provide rectangular windows through which to shoot. I talk through my idea with Matthew and he agrees, though his voice sounds a bit dazed. I don't know if it's from the abrupt halt to our kissing or his scepticism about my tactics. I don't ask.

My plan should work if there are only seven of them. If more have come, I don't know what we will do.

I squat behind the middle shelf, with a clear view of the door. My bow drawn.

'I'm ready,' I whisper and Matthew walks quietly across the room. He spins the huge metal wheel and quickly pulls the door open.

In the moonlight, I catch a glimpse of a creature, its mouth opening to reveal those sharpened teeth, before I let loose an arrow which slams into her heart.

The others screech and the next one who hovers in the doorway receives Matthew's knife, flung from his position. I am sure it only goes into the creature's shoulder but it's enough to make the feral fall back, into the darkness. We hear growling and can only hope they haven't fallen to feasting on the victims. We'll never be able to get past them, even with *that* as a distraction, I don't believe they'll be giving us up easily.

They were just trying to ... expand.

For a moment, there is quiet, no movement in the moonlight. Can they be planning something? I think I can hear the sound of something being dragged – maybe the one I hit – and then something comes flying through the air. It lands at my feet. A piece of something. Then a barrage of broken bits and pieces: chunks of cement, bits of metal. A crude attack or a planned distraction? There are still at least five of them out there.

I wipe my hands on my dress, trying to get rid of the sweat. I need to keep my arrow ready.

The flying things stop. Maybe the creatures think we have been wounded.

We wait. My eyes have adjusted rapidly to the changing light – one advantage of having lived my life with fire – and I can see the shapes of the creatures in the doorway. They are moving cautiously. They are not, it seems, completely without thought. There are three of them, huddled together and they make small, mewing noises.

When the front one steps forward into the room, we remain still. My fingers ache from holding onto the string of the bow. A wave of putridness comes with the ferals – the stink of unwashed flesh – and I have to fight back the desire to gag. I don't want them to know where I am yet.

The other two slink in, the three of them forming a triangle in front of the doorway. They couldn't have made it easier for us.

'Now,' I whisper to Matthew, and he jumps up to catch their attention.

They roar at him at the same time as my first arrow flies. I have fired without even thinking and caught the creature in the front, again directly into the heart. It pitches forward with a horrible scream. As if my fingers have been born to it, I re-load with an ease and quickness like I've never been able to before and dispatch the second of the creatures to the right, who has stood there, open-mouthed and confused during the death of the other.

The third creature roars and springs towards Matthew before I have time to take it out. Matthew has my knife and runs towards it with his own war cry. The two of them do a freakish dance in the grey light. This time, Matthew is prepared and barely a moment passes before the creature slumps to his feet, the blade sticking from its chest.

Five down. Two, and maybe, a half, to go.

Matthew and I retrieve the arrows and knife from the bodies. Matthew slings the bag full of ZarVex over his shoulder.

Will the other two creatures appear in the doorway and make my plan look like a perfect one?

We wait. Neither of them appear. They are not entirely stupid.

'Maybe the rest have run away?' Matthew whispers to me.

'Maybe.' For some reason, I don't feel confident. I remember the creature with the streak of black in his hair, the one who'd seemed to signal to the others. He's not amongst the dead.

'Now that we have air, maybe we should wait until the sun is fully up,' Matthew says.

It isn't a bad suggestion, except I'm not sure I can stand the thought of staying in this room, with three dead creatures, for any longer than necessary. No matter how much I try to remember they were *once like me.*

'We're due back at the bridge this morning. If we don't go now, we might not be able to meet up with the others.' Matthew is watching me, closely. 'And get back to the village quickly.'

I need him to understand this isn't about Bayat, but about getting home as soon as we can. What's the point of finding the ZarVex if we lose our way tracking back? He knows we have relied heavily on Bayat and Oyan's knowledge of the land, we can't risk losing one another.

'You're right.'

Carefully, we thread through the darkness of the sealed room, stepping over the bodies. I shiver as my foot brushes up against the skin of a leg.

In the main room, the beginning of dawn bathes everything in grey light and we see the body of the first creature I shot, a pile of rags next to the huge windows. I don't look too closely.

A more nauseating sight is the body of the creature Matthew threw his knife at. It lies in the centre of the room with its head partly cut off. They have slit his throat. The head sits with a red gash, its triangular teeth fixed into a grimace, forever tilted to the left.

I can't remember any screams to match this act.

'Why would they do this?' Matthew asks.

I think of wounded goats and the way in which they would be despatched quickly with a slit to the throat. An act of mercy. This isn't the time for hypothesising, though.

'They have your knife,' I point out instead.

Through the window of the first door I see one of the male creatures standing in front of the stairwell as a guard. It's not the one with the black streak in his hair.

I just begin to wonder where he is when I hear growling behind me. I turn to see him emerging from his hiding place, behind one of the benches. He seems to move quicker than the others, scurrying towards me, his mouth open for attack.

I raise my bow, aiming the arrow at his heart and, suddenly, he stops.

His mouth closes, his nose crinkles as if smelling me. His eyes are dead black, not orange like the others, though I can still see the long vertical pupil. At the end of his hands are the nails turned into claws, the rags which hang off his shoulders are hardly clothes, the white and black hair on his head is matted like fur, his skin is orange in patches or, now I see, patterns. He is no longer human. So why do I hesitate again?

The creature senses something, but he doesn't take advantage of my weakness and run at me. We stare at each other. He begins to back away, stumbling and then turning to sprint out the sixth door. I lower my bow.

We move into the corridor cautiously. Both the creatures have gone. Standing in their place is the old man.

'You can't take that.' He points at the bag.

'We need it,' I say. 'We don't even know if this will be enough.'

'I need it!'

He lunges at Matthew who pushes him away. I can tell Matthew is trying to be gentle, whilst still making sure the ZarVex is safe. The old man stumbles backwards, his scarf falls to the ground and we see his neck. Two red puncture wounds.

For a moment, all three of us are frozen. Then the man's hand jumps to his wound, trying to cover it up.

'Run Matthew!' I scream and we both rush to the stairwell. We sprint down the stairs, not knowing if the old man is following or not.

'The other ones are probably waiting to ambush us somewhere on the way!' Matthew yells. He might be right. I'm hoping not. I let him live and, for whatever reason, the creature with the black streak was grateful. Maybe they will come back here and feed on their former tribespeople. They will be content – whatever that means for them – for some time.

I'm more worried about the old man but when I pause for a moment and look up, I see him at the top of the stairs. He isn't coming after us.

I still keep my bow at the ready as we come out into the streets with the red sun just emerging on the horizon. In the light of sunrise the city looks almost, not quite, maybe ... something which might have been wonderful. There are less shadows and the concrete has a kind of glow. It can't compete with the beauty of a sunrise near the river, but it isn't all bad.

I feel outside of my body, as if I haven't just spent half the night in a sealed room with possibly cannibalistic creatures waiting nearby, as if I haven't just killed some of them, as if we still don't have a long and exhausting journey ahead of us.

The relief of being out in the open again. Fresh air.

'Pandora!' A shout comes from the top of the hill

and I know it can only be one person. Bayat.

He and Titus wave. I immediately start to run towards them, my quiver of arrows bouncing against my back, the string of my bow cutting into my torso.

'What happened to being quiet and unobserved?' Matthew asks sourly as he catches up with me.

We are with them in moments and I can't stop myself from throwing my arms around Bayat, burying my face into his neck. His arms grip me tightly. I take in the smell of him, his skin so beautiful compared to … no, I really don't want to think about the creatures right now.

'You're okay?' he asks, finally releasing me, holding me by the shoulders, running his eyes up and down me, checking for hurts.

'We're more than okay.' Matthew stands by my side, pulling the bag over his shoulders. 'We found ZarVex.'

The jeering in his words takes away any of the joy I thought I'd feel at sharing the news. As if this is all some childish competition, a game for attracting the most attention.

'You're kidding,' Titus says. He and Bayat watch silently as Matthew opens one of the boxes and shows the vials to them.

I am biting my tongue from pointing out it was

me who actually found them or telling them Matthew wouldn't have even gone into the white building if it hadn't been for my vision. But do I really need to play this game? This isn't about some of us being winners, or losers. This is about survival. About my father.

'That's amazing,' Bayat says. It sounds genuine, without a hint of envy. He isn't playing the game either.

19

Titus tells us they did find a hospital a fair way to the south but there seemed to be a group of ferals living there. He doesn't say it explicitly but I get the impression Titus wanted to go in and Bayat refused. They'd decided to come find us, to see if we might infiltrate it together. When he uses the word 'infiltrate' I can't help but smile, like we have some amazing abilities. I don't even want to begin to tell him about our encounters with the creatures, how completely hopeless we were most of the time.

'But, now, I guess we don't have to go back there.' Titus sounds disappointed.

Bayat is looking down into the bag of ZarVex. 'Do you think that's enough? For everyone?'

'We didn't exactly have time to count,' Matthew says, glancing at me.

'Why? What happened?'

I squint down the avenue to the harbour, the morning wind flows off the water and up to us. I feel cold and wish I'd brought Bayat's cloak with me, not left it with Fatima. Fatima. I wonder what she is doing right now. I hate to think of her alone. After encountering the creatures, I can't blame her for choosing to stay behind.

'You should have told us they don't stay dead unless you get their heart,' I say quietly. I don't want it to be an accusation, only a recognition of how he put us in danger.

'I told you to avoid them during this mission. At all costs.' His voice is hard.

'That wasn't possible,' Matthew counters. I realise this isn't strictly true. We didn't have to go into the art gallery or the white building. If we hadn't, though, we wouldn't have found the medicine. But maybe we would have found it anyway, in the hospital they saw. Maybe we didn't have to put ourselves at such risk. Either way, there is no point arguing about it now.

'We need to get back to the bridge to find Oyan and Emmaline,' I say instead.

We make our way back along the shoreline, scooting quickly past the art gallery, weapons at the ready, and come around under the concrete block holding up the bridge on this side. We climb up the embankment, clambering to almost exactly the spot where Matthew and I had landed on the road. At first, it looks like there's no sign of them. Then we hear a moan.

'Bayat?' Oyan's voice calls, though with none of its usual arrogance. If anything, he sounds scared. 'We're over here.'

They are on the far side of the bridge, crouched next to one of the huge steel girders. As we get closer, we can make out the dark shape of a body lying on the ground. The body moans again.

Emmaline's eyes are closed, her skin orange and sickly, just like the skin I have seen too often in the last day. On her left shoulder is an open wound where a piece of her flesh has been torn off, and two red puncture marks. Next to me, Titus turns and throws up.

'It came out of nowhere,' Oyan whimpers.

I expect Bayat to offer some words of comfort to his brother. Instead he stands up and turns to Titus, who is wiping his mouth on his vest.

'You need to go get Fatima and bring her back here as soon as you can.'

'Back here?' Titus asks. 'Aren't we going to her?'

Bayat shakes his head.

'I have another plan. Can you trust me?'

Titus hesitates for a moment, then nods.

'Matthew, you divide up the supplies.'

Matthew also nods and they move away from us, silently rifling through the bags to find water and food for Titus to take.

Emmaline makes a strange sound. For a moment, I think it is another blood-choked moan until I recognise it as the beginnings of a growl.

Titus says goodbye and begins the climb back over the bridge.

Oyan remains crouching, seemingly unable to move. I wonder how they escaped from the creature.

'We have to get her back to your village,' Bayat says quietly to me.

'She isn't going to last that long,' I reply, hardly raising my voice above a whisper. I don't know if Bayat has understood the full meaning of those wounds. 'She's going to become one of them.'

'What are you talking about?'

'Didn't you ever wonder how these creatures breed, Bayat?'

'She's just been hurt. We need to tend to it ...'

'This isn't something that is going to go away.'

Oyan suddenly stands up.

'Why are you arguing about this now? What does it matter? Look at her! Look at her!'

I ignore him, turning to Bayat again.

'We think the ferals were *made* and their condition can be passed on in blood. Yes, look at her.'

We look down at Emmaline. Her eyes open and they are completely black, with no sign of a pupil. I point to her hands where her fingernails have elongated. Her eyes close again.

'We have to get away from her.'

Even as I speak the words I can hardly believe I'm saying them. Emmaline, who I've known all my life. Beautiful and clever Emmaline who I've envied all my life. I just want to abandon her? Would I do the same if it was Bayat? Or Fatima? Or Matthew?

Now Matthew is kneeling beside her, reaching out a shaking hand to touch her forehead. He stops and turns his head towards me.

'If it's a blood condition then maybe ...'

Matthew stares at me, hoping I will understand, only my head is too full to comprehend.

'ZarVex?' he whispers it.

For a moment, I still don't get it. And then I do.

The old man ... that was why he was so unwilling to let us have the drug.

How haven't you been ... made ... to join them?

I have my ways.

Like the old man, maybe Emmaline can be saved before the virus takes hold.

I have to stop my hand from shaking as I stick the needle into the coating over the top of the vial. When my mother talked me through this, she did it in case she wouldn't be able to administer the drug when we got back to the village, though I don't want to think about that. But now I am thinking about it. *We cannot know the future.* What if we get back to a village already full of the dead? What if we've taken too long?

'Pandora, you need to concentrate.'

Bayat and Matthew are sitting on either side of me. I shake my head.

'I'm sorry.'

I tip the vial upwards, pulling the plastic end of the needle downwards, watching as the thin white liquid fills up the barrel. We have decided to use the maximum dosage the needle allows, given we have no real way of knowing if it will make a difference. I am nervous about using so much, when we don't know how much we'll need when we get home, but there isn't much choice.

Carefully, I carry the full needle to her. Oyan is cradling her head on his knees. He doesn't seem to be afraid of what she might become. Or perhaps he doesn't believe me. Bayat and Matthew follow, like a procession.

'Hold her arm,' I tell Oyan. I don't know if she can still feel pain but I don't want her jerking away before we get the stuff into her.

I breathe in. I've never done anything like this before. I half laugh to myself. What difference does that make? When I think of all I have done, for the first time, since leaving the village …

I breathe out and stick the needle into the crook of Emmaline's arm. I aim for what I think is a line of blue, though I'm not sure. The thin tip pops into her flesh. A small drop of blood bubbles up. Emmaline doesn't even flinch and as I push the plunger in, sending the drug into her system, I hope we are not too late.

We bind up the torn flesh with strips made from the bottom of her dress. I feel better when the two red wounds are out of sight.

'You guard her, Oyan,' Bayat directs and then gestures to me and Matthew.

We make our way down to the water again – Bayat and me with bow and arrow at the ready, Matthew with a drawn knife – and Bayat talks about his idea of sailing home. How he has seen boats, in the distance, along the shore.

I have seen pictures of boats. In our library there was a volume called *The Art of Sailing,* which had once belonged to Stratum, filled with pictures of dinghies, canoes and yachts. I remember he pointed to the diagrams showing the way in which the boats tracked the wind and sighed wistfully, like he would've given anything to be doing exactly that again. I didn't have any such longing. It had simply been another curiosity, another part of life before The Burning which I assumed I would never get to experience. But as we walk along the land's edge – the water lapping hard up against the stone wall that still stands in places, though collapsed in more – I feel the thrill of thinking that I might go out on the sea.

Bayat is talking about how much easier it would

be to go up the coast, rather than travelling back inland, how we could cut our return journey in half, especially given Emmaline's condition. Matthew is arguing back about how we could also get completely lost, or wrecked, or drowned.

I don't really listen too hard. I already know whose side I'm on and not just because I'm naturally inclined toward Bayat's point of view. I prefer to take the risk. Besides, I can't see the point in arguing about something which is still a pretty remote possibility. First, we have to find a boat that's actually in one piece.

We are travelling along a pathway of dry dirt. We traverse a huge crater, the clearest sign of a bomb attack we've seen and follow the U shape of the harbour, as it cuts into the remaining land.

Around the edge of the jutting peninsula, we spy what we're looking for: about fifty feet below us is a huge wooden jetty lined with sailing ships. They're not lined up neatly in rows, like in the pretty pictures I've seen: it is a huge pile of entangled poles and overturned boats. I count up to thirty of them, thrown against each other like crushed bodies. They have not, by the look of it, been bombed, just swept into this mess by giant waves.

Bayat stands, stricken. I want to say something

reassuring. It *was* a good idea, just maybe a bit optimistic.

'Well, that was a waste of energy,' Matthew says, somewhat spitefully.

'We should at least go down and double-check,' I suggest and start to climb down the embankment, walking sideways to brace myself against the sliding ground.

Up close, the state of the boats becomes even clearer. None of them are without damage. They are really just floating garbage.

I walk away from the pile, towards the end of the jetty, leaving Bayat to continue to point to one boat after another, 'that one might be okay', only to be mocked by Matthew, 'except it has a huge hole in its front'.

Half of the path has fallen or rotted away, the smell from the water is stronger here, just like the freshness which comes off our river in the early morning. I look down and watch it lap against the pylon.

I hear a scream, almost the same as Matthew and I had heard before. Except it's coming from the other side of the harbour.

The two boys run to stand next to me.

'What do you think it was?' Bayat asks solemnly.

In the distant sky, I can see something flying towards us. It has white wings, flapping against the grey clouds. About half way across the water, it lets out another scream, its beak screeching wide.

The bird flies over our heads and we all follow its flight along the length of the jetty before it lands on one of the broken, upturned boats, its webbed feet clumsy on the slippery slope.

I let out a small laugh. The sight of the bird, I'm pretty sure it's called a seagull, has only brought home how confused we are in this strange place.

I go to turn away from this reminder of our lack of knowledge and, in doing so, catch a glimpse of something under the jetty, at the shoreline. We have focused so much on the obvious, we haven't let ourselves see what might be hidden.

An intact boat, bobbing under the wharf, next to a thin strip of sandy shore. Somehow it has managed to avoid being caught up in the destruction of the rest.

Bayat gawps at it like it's something from a dream

and even Matthew's former sourness is touched by the beauty of it.

'*By the rivers ...*' he begins and then says nothing more.

We pull at the muddy rope tying the boat to a round, metal hook in the stone wall, the three of us trying to drag it closer to shore. We don't want it getting stuck in the mud but we also don't want to jump on and find it sinking beneath our feet in deep water. We wade in up to our waists. The question of how to get into it is another one altogether.

'Here.' Bayat links his two hands together below the water line, offering me a leg up. He smiles. 'Come on, you're the lightest.'

I grin back.

'Sure, and I guess I'll be the wettest if it sinks.'

'I'll rescue you,' he counters. 'I promise.'

I place my foot into his palm, putting my hands on his shoulders. He hoists me up, I twist around and grab the edge of the boat with both hands. The whole thing begins to tip towards me and I think I'm going to capsize it but I hear Bayat grunt, pushing my feet up from below. I half tumble, half somersault aboard.

My head bangs against the side, but not hard. I sit up and climb onto the bench seat embedded on one side, feeling the bob and tug of the water below. It is like nothing I've ever felt before. This strange sense of being on solid ground and being completely afloat. Not all of the floor is totally solid, mind you, there are holes where the material – is it wood? no, it feels different from that – has given way. It lists a little to the left as I lean over, yet there are no signs of it collapsing and water doesn't seem to be coming in.

I peer down at Matthew and Bayat. My smile says enough for them to help each other aboard.

The boat has two sails, a large one and a small one, both of which have been wound up. When we unfurl them, there are holes in them which have been sewn up – by who? – and, though Matthew thinks the joins look flimsy and breakable, Bayat argues they will be strong enough to catch the wind. I can't name what type of boat it is. Not a yacht, maybe a dinghy? I can't remember, but it will hold seven of us – three on one side, four on the other. Not comfortably, but we can definitely make our way home quicker, if the wind will take us.

We return to Oyan. Emmaline is no different, although she does seem, at least, to be no worse. Her eyes remain closed and she makes no more growling sounds.

Bayat hands out supplies of berries and dried rabrat. I'm famished and everything – the water, the bread, the tiny green berries and the meat – has the most intense flavour.

'The taste of being alive,' Matthew says and I smile and nod. Yes, that's why it seems so fantastic because, not long ago, there'd been the possibility we'd never have the chance to eat or drink again.

Matthew and I still don't tell our story and I am getting more nervous about how I will tell that tale. Kaplan and the vision. Matthew and the kiss. Letting the creature with the black streak go. Already I can feel the need to keep certain things secret from Bayat. Would he actually forgive me the kiss, since we were under such stress? And was that the only reason I kissed Matthew? I hate the fact I've got stories I don't want to tell Bayat. My delay in telling him Matthew was my Chosen has already made him suspicious of me. Will he ever trust me again if I don't tell him everything that happened? And if he finds out some other way? Would Matthew be jealous enough to boast about our embrace? Oh yes, that isn't hard to imagine ...

I feel the quiet, the frustration of having nothing to do.

'What's taking Titus and Fatima so long?' I complain. 'We need to get out of here.'

'We just have to wait it out,' Matthew says and, for once, Bayat nods in agreement. 'We can't leave them behind.'

'How can we just sit around when we have the stuff to save everyone?' I stand up and pace up and down. 'What if we get back and find out they've died only a few hours before? The hours we were waiting here?' The thought makes my stomach turn again.

'If we don't make it back, we'll never even know when they died,' Bayat says.

I throw myself back onto the ground and sit with my head in my hands.

We wait.

We agree to take turns to sit with Emmaline throughout the night. Bayat insists on taking the first shift.

We have moved to the slightly softer ground of the embankment and Bayat gives me his almost empty bag to use as a pillow. I lie, curled up, at Emmaline's feet. Matthew and Oyan are lying on either side of her, whilst Bayat sits cross-legged at her head. It's like a circle of protection around her and I can only hope any threat will come from outside, not from within her.

When I close my eyes I feel the deep fatigue I've been fighting off for so long. A series of images flash inside my head: the boat floating on the water, the gaping red wound on Emmaline's shoulder, the female creature's face just before I shot her. Then the jumble becomes too much and there is blackness and, finally, sleep.

20

It is light when I wake up and I realise the boys haven't woken me to do my guard duty. Maybe I should be annoyed by this, only I can't bring myself to be. My neck is aching badly and when I sit up, the bones in my legs crack. I turn my head to see Bayat sitting where he was last night, at Emmaline's head, except now his face has a smile on it. He looks at me and then down at Emmaline's body and I understand why he is happy.

Her skin is back to a rosy pink and her breathing is one of normal, deep sleep.

I burst into tears.

'Hey! Hey!' Bayat scrambles over to put his arms around me. I cry into his shoulder, unable to stop myself sobbing. The relief of knowing Emmaline isn't going to turn into a feral has unwound my whole body, like a plug has been removed that was holding me vaguely together.

'It's okay,' Bayat whispers into my hair. He doesn't seem to think it strange I'm weeping at the time when we should be celebrating. He pats me on the back as if I'm a young one.

Gradually, my tears run out. Bayat continues to hold me and we sit, silently, watching as the city is bathed in morning rays. The sky has returned to blue and, again, it is almost beautiful. If it wasn't for the battered, grey wreckage scattered on the streets.

'Where are Oyan and Matthew?' I ask at last not really wanting to break the moment.

'They went to get the boat.'

'Really?'

He nods.

'Why didn't you go?'

He shrugs. I wonder what kind of argument he had to have with Matthew to get his way this time.

'I thought you might want to tell me about how you found the ZarVex.'

I feel myself turn red.

'What did Matthew say?'

'He said you led him to a building because of something you heard in your vision.'

I know I have been unkind to Matthew, again,

thinking he would tell Bayat about our kiss out of spite.

'Yes, the cougar spoke to me. But, before she did, the cougar was … you.'

Bayat frowns.

'Why would that be?' he asks.

'Caro told me your visions make you a great hunter. That *you* see the cougar.'

He shakes his head.

'No, that's not what I've seen.'

'What then?'

Bayat looks out to the water. He has the same expression on his face as when I told him about my dream of thousands, a kind of fury about being made to think of the past.

'My first came when I was very young, too young for me to be able to remember details, but somehow I do.'

His brown eyes focus on me. He breathes out, as if forcing himself to let go of the anger.

'My mother was … intense. We were at her work, the one time we went there. My father was sick and he had to stay home in bed and my mother, she was so angry about having to take us with her. Only we had no one else. We travelled in one of the underground trains – they called them 'bullets' and we thought this was so cool – being in a bullet. The sound it made, the world rushing by like we'd been shot out of a gun.

'When we got there, it was all guards with machine guns and steel doors and my mother striding through corridors with the same fierceness she did everything. I was trembling by the time we got into the lab. She told us she couldn't do anything important while we were there so we'd have to stay in the office next door. We spent a lot of time swirling each other around in a chair on wheels. It was fun.

'Oyan fell asleep and I was bored. I crept out of the office. The lab was empty, my mother nowhere to be seen. I went out into the corridor. There was this smell. I don't know if I'd noticed it before only now it was just overwhelming. I guess I kind of followed it, even if that sounds stupid.'

I shrug, not wanting to break the stream of words.

'There was a room full of cages. Each contained a big cat. Mainly cougars. But also a jaguar and some snow leopards. And a tiger, even though they were supposed to be extinct. I stood in that prison and I realised the smell was feline fear.'

'What were they doing with them?'

'I don't know. I went up to the tiger and stood

as close as I dared. She was sick. I could feel her pain. She looked into my eyes and I don't remember anything for a while.'

'You had a vision?'

'Yes, but I don't know what was in it. I remember feeling like I was floating in the night sky, nothing more. I came out of it when my mother found me. At first, she seemed angry, telling me off for being there, for leaving my brother. Then it was like she realised I'd had some connection with the animal and she started drilling me with questions. How had it happened? What did I see? I felt too sick to answer and I ended up throwing up on her.'

I think back to my vision. This is how he knew about how physically bad I would feel after.

'That night, she came into our bedroom to say goodnight, something she never usually did. It was always my father. But this night she came and sat on the edge of my bed. Oyan had already fallen asleep but I hadn't been able to get the tiger's eyes out of my head.'

I knew that feeling.

'My mother also had the most amazing green eyes and it was like the two of them – tiger and human – had melded together somehow. She told me how glad she was I'd come with her to work that day because now she knew how special I was. And how helpful I could be.'

'What did she mean?'

'I don't know. The next day my father took us away, to the mountains.'

'But he didn't stay with you?'

'No.'

His face is hard again and I know he isn't going to tell me more.

In the silence, we look at Emmaline. Is it my imagination or is the skin on her arms slightly orange again? Bayat doesn't say anything so I think it must be a trick of the light.

'They will be back soon, Pandora. We should eat.'

I chew on my last piece of bread, constantly distracted by watching the turn in the harbour. I am so keen to catch the first glimpse of the boat in sail I barely taste the food, even though my stomach is hungry for it.

Emmaline is still sleeping and we decide not to wake her, letting her rest for as long as she can. I'm not particularly looking forward to telling her what she's been through, so the more we can delay, the better.

After we've finished our breakfast, there is nothing really to do except wait. Bayat decides to sit and count the vials of ZarVex, just so we have an idea of how to divide it between my village and his tribe. I don't respond when he says this, because it reminds me of what is coming when we return home.

I stand a little distance away from him and Emmaline, trying to act as a guard. I scan the bridge, recalling Oyan's words – 'it came out of nowhere' – and, to my surprise, I think I do see a figure on the opposite shore. Not a creature, though. Someone, shrouded in black, who ducks out of sight just as I look. Or is it just a shadow?

A moment later there is definitely someone there. Waving, his blonde hair blowing in the wind. Titus.

'Bayat, Titus is back!'

He closes the bag of vials and stands up. The two of us watch as Titus traverses the metal girders. He moves as quickly as he can – though he has at least three bags and, I notice, my cloak slung over his shoulder – scurrying along the edge as if there isn't a watery threat below, as if he isn't being buffeted by the harbour swirls.

When he jumps onto the concrete road, he is panting, sweat runs down his forehead. I voice the question which has been in my head since the moment I saw him.

'Where's Fatima?'

Fatima is gone. This is what Titus tells us when he recovers his breath.

'All our bags were still there, except hers. I brought back as much as I could carry. They're on the other side. We'll have to go back and bring them over in a few trips.'

'What do you mean gone?' I can't believe he is trying to move onto other things so quickly.

'Gone, Pan. She wasn't there. I called out and travelled up the highway for a long time, shouting her name.'

'But she knew to wait. It hasn't been four days.'

'Maybe she got scared.'

I can't deny Fatima would have been afraid, alone out there. But would she really have tried to return home? Leaving all our things? Abandoning us? I can't believe that of her.

'What if something happened to her? What if one of the creatures ...?'

'We haven't seen them on that side of the bridge,'

Bayat interrupts. 'I don't think they live over there. They probably can't move that way.'

This doesn't make sense, the ferals looked completely capable of climbing the bridge.

'We have to go and find her!'

'I searched, Pan, I really did!' Titus is yelling at me.

'What are you saying? We're just going to leave her here?' I'm yelling back. I knew Titus didn't have proper feelings for Fat. How could he be so willing to forget about her?

Bayat is shaking his head and Titus has just noticed Emmaline's supine body.

'Is Emmaline okay now?' Titus is looking at her hands. She still has long nails.

Bayat doesn't answer him. Surely he will say that we'll go looking? That there is no way he is going to leave Fatima behind?

'I'm really sorry Pan, but I think we have to focus on getting back to the tribe and your village,' Bayat speaks in a quiet voice but his words fill me with fury.

'No!'

Before I can protest more we hear voices calling to us.

'Bayat! Pan!'

Around the jutting finger of the land below, the boat, its sails spluttering, suddenly appears. Oyan and Matthew are screaming at us, pointing in the direction of the art gallery.

Ferals. The same group Matthew and I first encountered, though I count only ten. They are on the other side of the road, moving as a group towards the embankment, their slow stealthy gait the reason we had not even noticed them.

Titus grabs a bow and starts to clumsily notch the arrow. I reach for my bow as well.

'No!' Bayat screams at us. 'We have to get to the boat.'

'We can fight them!' Titus insists.

'We have what we came for,' Bayat speaks shakily. 'We don't need to kill them.'

Titus raises his bow, aiming at the distant creatures. I know he wants to prove himself. But Bayat is right, we can escape.

I put down my bow and start to scramble our things together.

'Titus, carry Emmaline! I'll take as many bags as I can. Bayat, you take the weapons.'

Titus stares down the length of his bow for a moment. He sighs, throws it down in frustration and kneels to scoop Emmaline up.

We sprint down to the harbour. Titus has slung Emmaline over his shoulder and I have three bags and my cloak bouncing all around me. Bayat has the bag of ZarVex and as many bows and arrows as he can manage.

Matthew and Oyan have tried to manoeuvre the boat near the bottom of a set of stone steps running into the water but they don't seem to have much control over it. The smaller sail has come loose and is flapping uselessly. They are not close enough for us to jump abroad.

I start tossing bags at them, trying not to panic. We will need these supplies.

'Catch this!'

Bayat throws the bag of ZarVex and I watch breathlessly as it soars across the space and is caught by Matthew. He looks green enough already and goes even greener when he realises what he's just received.

'Where's Fatima?' he calls out, hugging the bag to his chest.

'She's gone!' Titus yells back, as if he's angry Matthew has dared to ask.

'Gone?'

'We can't get any closer!' Oyan shouts. 'You'll have to swim!'

'We'll take Emmaline between us,' I urge Titus. I suspect I am a stronger swimmer than Bayat who's hanging back from the water.

'You go,' I say to him. He steels himself and jumps in. He emerges a moment later and begins to paddle slowly towards the boat.

Titus follows with Emmaline on his shoulder. He bobs up and turns onto his back, trying to float her but I can see how heavy she is, the water hasn't woken her and her legs drag down.

I am on the bottom step, still with the cloak around me. I know I will have to leave it behind, its weight will be too heavy to swim with.

I hear growling behind me. At the top of the stairs, a male feral stands, its mouth wide open and hideous.

'Pan!' Matthew cries.

I don't have any weapon. The creature is slinking down the steps towards me. I crouch down, in my cloak, as if I might be able to hide. The feral does not stop. There is nothing left in this creature. No caution. No fear. No humanity.

I glance out to the boat. Bayat has got there and Titus is also close, dragging Emmaline through the water. Matthew and Oyan scramble around, trying to figure out a way to turn.

'Don't come back!' I shout. They can't risk being taken by the ferals. They can't risk the ZarVex. I realise I'm not afraid of death, if I know my parents will be saved, if I know the village will go on. So, in the end, maybe I can be brave.

I turn to face the creature. He continues down the stairs towards me and I run my fingers along the cougar fur of my cloak, feeling its warmth.

LETTERS

4

My dearest Pan,

Where are you? How far away are you now? Have you found the medicine? Are you safe? How torturous it is not knowing what is happening to you. Even more so, given how much we need you here.

Yesterday we lost Barone, LeeYin's husband – leaving Freya and Fee to be fatherless – and Thomas and Theseus, our youngest losses yet. The rest of the sick are struggling. We don't know how much longer any of them will last. We are all desperately tired. I have only forced myself to wake up and write to you because I feel as if my plea for you to come home might reach you, if the words are locked onto a page.

I shouldn't doubt you are trying your very best to get back to us. I shouldn't doubt how strong you are. It's only my fear and desperation talking.

Shall I go on with the story of our escape from the city? Perhaps it will distract me.

We had crossed the bridge and were driving silently through the outer areas, towards the barricades. I had no idea what we were planning and simply obeyed when Omar told Hector and me to put on our white lab coats.

'Just let Omar and me do all the talking,' Petty instructed and I nodded my agreement. I didn't think my voice would work anyway. I felt sick with fear.

The boundary of the city ended abruptly. The houses simply stopped and the road was lined with rolls of barbed wire. Enormous light poles illuminated the ground below, making the interior of the car a glowing capsule moving towards the triangular guard house and boom gate, painted with red and white stripes. Only two men, though both with machine guns, peering curiously at us. I remember one had a moustache, the other remains faceless. I was too afraid to look closely.

It was the moustached man who tapped on the window. Omar slid it down hesitantly, as if he couldn't understand what the problem might be.

'You goin' somewhere?' the guard asked, leaning

against the roof of the car, his gun dangling casually over his shoulder. He might have thought we were the 'joy-riders' they talked about, rich kids with nothing better to do than cruise around the boundaries.

Omar nodded his head back at us in the passenger seats.

'Gotta take the professors to the Brownback Institute. Top secret or somethin'.' His accent was completely different to how he'd spoken before. I could barely believe it was the same person.

'We didn't get told about it.' The guard glanced at Petty. 'And what's she got to do with it?'

'Can't expect a man to go travelling alone into the dead-lands.'

'Maybe on the way back, honey,' Petty's voice had also changed completely, 'we might have time for a bit of fun?'

I sucked in air, trying not to let my distress show.

The guard smiled.

'They don't tell me shit 'round here.'

The other guard was already walking back to the box.

'The terminal's on the blink anyway. Just let the docs through.'

The guard looked again at Petty. He stood back, gripping his gun with both hands. I was terrified he was going to demand his 'fun' right there and then.

'See ya soon,' he said. The boom gate opened and I was amazed at how slowly Omar was able to make himself drive through the lit border into the darkness. Into freedom.

No one spoke for quite a long time. We didn't want to test our luck.

We were travelling along a highway, a road that, long ago, would have led to small towns but which had become dead land when the shrinking populace moved to the city. In the night, the weak lights of the car barely illuminated a few feet ahead of us and I had no real sense of what was out there. As dawn approached, I saw valleys and hills covered in trees, multi-layered hues of green and heard the first morning cries of birds, and wondered how anyone could call it dead.

'What is the Brownback Institute?' Hector finally asked, breaking the silence. We had gone far enough to feel like we might be safe.

'I don't know,' Omar replied. 'I've heard rumours of places outside the boundaries where they do government research on animals. I figured the guards would have too.'

'You based your entire plan on a rumour?' I thought of the machine guns and the whisper-thin protection we had had.

'If the lady is dissatisfied, she could always find another ride,' Petty quipped.

We fell silent once more. Hector found my hand again, and squeezed it, trying to reassure me.

'I'm sorry, Omar, I didn't mean to sound ungrateful.'

'It's okay,' he said, though he didn't sound as if it was.

'I've never been in a situation like this before,' I tried to explain.

'What sort of situations have you been in?' Petty demanded.

'What do you mean?'

'Tell us about your childhood, Zaana. Where you were born.'

I looked over to Hector. He was shaking his head.

'She doesn't have to justify herself to you Petty.'

I didn't want this to be my relationship with Petty, already this animosity. I'd had so few women of my own age in my life, I naively thought we might be friends.

'I was born in the North. My parents had a sustainable farm in Sun Valley. I don't remember it. By the time I was five, the changes in the climate had made it unsustainable. Like everyone else, we moved to Melney.'

That was all I would tell them. They didn't need to

know how my parents had sold out, betraying their neighbours in signing over their land to the miners, allowing them a foothold which would spread across the valley until it was one, gaping, dead hole, unable to bear life of any kind. How my parent's blood money would allow them to become lazy and uncaring.

We passed over an enormous steel bridge, shaped like three turtle backs. The highway veered sharply upwards and the car slowed down, its engine fading out at the bottom of the hill. Hector tried to get it going again, pressing the kick-start button. Its battery had died, though, and there was nowhere to re-charge it.

'End of the line, folks.' Petty opened her door, stretching out her long boots, unwinding herself from the seat like an unfurling flower.

I pushed my door open and almost fell onto the ground, my legs heavy and awkward.

When Omar emerged, I realised how foolish my earlier comment had been. His entire body was bathed in sweat and his eyes looked like they were going to pop out of his head. There had been nothing casual or offhand about his plan. He had, clearly, put his heart and soul into it.

We unpacked the car. We had camping equipment and enough supplies for two weeks. The idea was to walk into the forest and attempt to link up with one of the subsistence settlements we had heard of, via more rumours. When I look back, I still wonder at our trust in unconfirmed ideas.

It might have been as easy as that. I could tell you how we trundled along the river-bank and eventually found Theodore and Tareen with Atticus and Corrine, the founding couples of our village, already living in the huts you know so well, already growing their own food and raising goateeps, already perfecting all the methods which would help the River People thrive.

That is one story.

But it forgets the fire ball and the mud and the terror.

Every society likes to have its founding myth and Theodore did love his poetry.

Tossed amongst the world at last

Dream, but not of wonders past...

I haven't looked back, Pan, not because of 'wonders past' but because I hated to remember those days.

We had divided everything up, almost equally. I could see how Hector had smuggled some more weight into his backpack, to lighten mine. I might have protested, except I struggled enough to lug my pack over my shoulders and couldn't imagine being able to walk if it was any heavier. The four of us stood at the edge of the road, looking down the embankment we would have to scale to travel alongside the river. It was about midday.

I saw a flash of light, then heard a roaring sound, like a giant wave echoing in our eardrums. The horizon turned a volcanic red and we watched, horrified, as an enormous ball of fire travelled along the highway towards us. The heat blasted us first, throwing us onto the ground.

'Move!' Petty screamed. She flung off her backpack and scrambled down the embankment. I did the same, hardly registering where Hector or Omar were. I slid and fell through the grass, landing on all fours in the mud. I felt Hector's arms pick me up around the waist and place me back on my feet.

'Run!' he shouted and I stumbled after Petty and Omar who were already pelting along the riverbank. I didn't think we could outrun it and expected any moment to be engulfed by the flames. I didn't look back, pushing my muscles to work as hard as they had ever done in their life.

It was the river that saved us. *By the rivers*, as we say. Though the strange, sweeping fire made it over the bridge, it did not take hold of the damp forest, the body of water stopping it from laying waste to the trees on this side.

We didn't stop running, though, until night fell. We pushed ourselves on, Petty yelling at me when I tried to rest.

'Do you want us all to die?'

Hector too exhausted to tell her off.

When darkness came – though it was no longer a true night for the sky on the horizon was still lit red and it glowed enough not to let blackness fall – I just couldn't go any further.

I sat on a fallen log and hung my head.

'You can go on without me.'

Hector, who had been urging me on from behind, stopped too. He sat next to me. We didn't touch, it didn't seem the right thing to do.

Omar threw himself onto the sodden grass of the shoreline, with a groan. Petty stopped and stood, her hands on her hips. Her boots were caked in mud, her tank top streaked with dirt, her hair a wild mass. She panted, leaning over to catch her breath.

When she straightened, she focused on the vermillion glow, which made us all look in that direction. My home, my life, my parents. Gone.

'Talk about timing ...' Petty said.

We knew what she meant. If we had only delayed a day, we would have been in the city when what we would come to call The Burning came. We would have joined the thousands destroyed by that fire.

'Pity we didn't leave a few days earlier,' Hector said. 'Then we might still have our supplies.'

Our timing had been good, just not perfect.

We walked for four, or five, or six days. As Omar said to you, it wasn't a time for keeping track. We were in a daze, without any real food – we foraged for berries, which gave us stomach cramps – and were only saved by the fresh water we stumbled upon.

We didn't know if we would find any settlement and our survival skills were almost non-existent. Hector and Petty talked of setting traps, to catch rabrats or any other small animal stupid enough to get ensnared. I remained silently sceptical. Or I was just too exhausted to imagine what we would do to a captured creature, if we fluked it, with no knives. We had no fires. The wood was too damp and we had left our matches behind. We huddled together at night: Hector and I; Omar and Petty. The four of us. Even as we sat, entwined, I felt horribly alone.

It probably isn't worth dwelling on the misery of that time. As you know, we did find Theodore and his family and we were welcomed, along with the trickle of escapees who had come before, and survivors who would come after. The makings of our village. I know you never warmed to Theodore, Pan, but you cannot imagine the relief seeing his face brought to us. We were willing to do anything for him. He saved our lives.

Not to say those first few years were easy. I had lived my life, essentially, in isolation. First with my parents, then with Ivan. Now I was amongst people, all the time. And a people who wanted, who believed desperately, in the need to create a community. To name ourselves, to brand ourselves, to mark our growth with strange rituals. Even harder, everyone knowing one another's business.

The first three years were a new life of growing vegetables, learning how to cook, being shown how to feed, milk and kill goateeps. Day after day of discovering how everything I had taken for granted – food, clothes, clean water, shelter – had to be worked for, made and maintained. Nothing new to you, Pan, this is how it has always been. For me, it was like another world, like stepping onto another planet.

I admit I struggled. I remember one night, when we saw two celestial bodies – Venus and Jupiter – lined up in the sky together, shining brighter than I had ever seen them before, and all I could think was of how much I wanted to leave this place, this collection of hovels. Yes, I know, the hut has been your home and you would hate to hear me call it this but when you compare it to the apartment I used to dwell in … I just wanted to fly away. To join the stars and float, without fear or pain, in the Milky Way.

It was Hector who saved me, who kept me on the ground, who stopped me from ghosting. Your father worked hard to make life easier for me, even though he could never really embrace Theodore's ways. Hector was … is … practical. He wants to get on with doing things, not talk about them. Theodore, I knew, reminded him too much of Ivan.

At the end of the third year, when the adults had all been properly branded with the symbol of the River People, Theodore decided we needed to breed. I hate to tell this story, Pan, because you might feel its coldness. I still vividly recall the meeting, in the

Great Hall, in which the news was told to us.

'We are not special. We are just survivors,' we intoned, as we had been taught to do from the first.

'Survivors, yes. But for how long?' Theodore stood in front of the fire-pit. It was winter and the flames rising from the circle of stones were a vivid backdrop. With his beard, Theodore reminded me of the wizards in stories from my childhood. 'We have a responsibility to continue the human race.'

'Do we?' Hildur interrupted. This was just like her. She and her husband, Patrick, had arrived over a year ago, with their twin toddlers strapped to their backs. They didn't want to talk of where they had been since The Burning. 'What good has the human race ever done for this earth? We'd be better off letting ourselves die out.'

'How can you say that?' Tareen protested. 'As a mother?'

Hildur shrugged, her grey hair falling over her face.

'It's because I am a mother, I can say it. Why bring more children into a world without hope?'

'I have hope,' Theodore pronounced, his voice ringing out into the hall so strongly Hildur sat down and said nothing more. 'We are living a beautiful life here. It might be tough, at times. During winter, we are cold and hungry but in the spring, we are warm and full. This is the cycle and we have a duty to pass on our new way of living, at one with the seasons, without waste or greed for things which have no value.'

'This spring,' Tareen stood up next to Theodore, her soft tone contrasting with her husband's declamations, 'the women shall choose their partner, remove their implants and try to start new growth within them.'

'How romantic,' Petty whispered to me and I had to stop myself from giggling.

The implants were long, thin plastic strips placed under the skin of our arms. I had had a new one inserted just before leaving the city, and had another two years of protection from it. Did I really want to take it out this early? Did I really have Theodore's hope in my heart?

Of course, there was no question of partners. Hector and I were ... are ... in love and we had to decide, together, if we wanted to follow the edict. There was no notion of being forced, you should understand, only the pressure we felt to go along with what was best for the village.

Petty didn't want to have children, she told me

when we were playing at being friends. She wasn't afraid, like me, of the act of giving birth, she just hated the thought of being tied so completely to another human being. Her relationship with Omar was on and off, off and on. Whenever he became too full on, as she called it, Petty would ghost for a few days. We didn't know where she went, she'd turn up again and slip back into her chores, as if nothing had happened.

Still, we both became pregnant. As did Tareen, Corrine and Whisper. A springtime of fertility, the five of us growing our bellies, trundling around like a set of Russian dolls, each of us expanding at different phases of the moon so we could hardly believe we were due around the same time. I didn't grow as large as the others, and worried the baby wasn't forming properly. Ravena reassured me this was probably not the case.

'We all have different bodies,' she said. 'Yours is just naturally smaller than the rest of them.'

I tried not to envy Petty's wonderfully rotund stomach, especially because she was less than happy with it.

'When can I get this parasite out of me?' she moaned and I couldn't raise a smile at this horrible description of her growing baby.

If I tried to talk to Hector about how unexcited Petty was about the coming child, he told me things would be better when the child arrived, and changed the subject. I should've noticed how reluctant he was to discuss Petty.

I'd like to say the day of your birth was sunny and beautiful, Pan. It wasn't. Autumn had come and the skies were ominously grey. I was the first of the five to feel the labour pains and they, and Ravena, sat with me in the Great Hall, watching over the waves of agony, trying to guide me through the strain and push.

Three times I whispered 'I can't do this' and three times I heard Petty's strong voice come back at me 'yes, you can'.

I could. I did.

You, Pan, lay in my arms, bloodied but perfect.

After the cord had been cut, the men joined us: Theodore, beaming; Atticus, quietly happy; Omar, grabbing Petty's hand and kissing it and, for once, her smiling; Bren wrapping his arms around Whisper's belly and Hector, laying his head on my shoulder, gazing down on your head.

'For all the screaming,' Theodore said, 'we

thought The Burning had come again.'

I was glad to see a smile on his face, or else I would have taken it as criticism.

'Yes, and we wouldn't want to be reminded of that, would we?' Petty quipped.

A silence fell. This kind of flippancy wasn't common, especially when it came to Theodore's grand vision of our history and our future.

'We shall name her for the first woman created in antiquity and as a reminder of what evil there is in the world,' Theodore continued, as if Petty hadn't spoken. 'She shall be called Pandora.'

We had planned to name you after Hector's mother, Helen. I looked to him, expecting him to speak up in protest. He gave a small shake of the head and I knew it was hopeless. At the same moment, Tareen cried out that her time had come and the focus shifted to the birthing of Emmaline.

I lay, with you, next to Tareen as she went through her agony. The men had all scurried out and Ravena took over, sitting behind Tareen, as she had done with me, wrapping her legs around her to provide the support she needed. I was still too exhausted to do much except hold Tareen's hand, my other arm cradling you.

How can I tell you the rest? You would have heard

that Tareen didn't survive the birth. Emmaline was facing the wrong way and she had to be cut from the womb. More screams. Tareen died almost immediately after. I say 'almost' because there was a moment I still dread to remember, the moment when Tareen's hand gripped mine, her head turned towards me, her eyes fixed on the baby in my arms. *Your* eyes opened, your tiny brown orbs startlingly alive as you watched the life drain out of Emmaline's mother. I could have sworn you seemed to know what was happening.

I have never told you this story because, as with so much else, I worried how this knowledge of the past might affect you, how being so close to death on your first day of life may have seeped into you ...

In the next two weeks, Matthew was born to Petty, Fatima to Whisper and Titus to Corrine. They were all able to name their own children. Only you, as the first, was christened by Theodore, his grief over Tareen making him careless of the rest.

A year later, Matthew's brother, Christophe, was born and Fatima's sister, Cassie. Corrine and I were not so lucky, although neither of us could truly despair, having the joy of our one child. I also couldn't admit to anyone how Tareen's death had made me scared of falling pregnant again. I didn't attend any of the other births, hiding away, using you as my excuse. Hector didn't push me and loved you with a passion that came with knowing this was his only chance of loving a child.

I could almost stop now. You know what the rest is, Pan. That life continued in the village and we tried our best to raise you in a way which would bring sporadic happiness, even if we couldn't guarantee it at all times.

I need to sleep. I am so tired. And this retreat into the past makes the present even more painful. To remember Hildur and her two boys, as red-haired toddlers splashing in the mud and Whisper, laughing with relief as Fatima slid out into the world, and Corrine, crying when the pains came too early, Titus sucking his thumb next to the blood on the floor. Such a mess of memories, good and bad.

Pan, Pandora. How I miss you. Come home to me, soon,

Your mother,

Zaana

Part Five

21

I close my eyes and see my mother. She is on her knees in one of the fields, planting seedlings and I am running up to show her a snail-shell. She smiles and traces her finger along the perfect spiral.

I hear the growl.

I squeeze my eyes tightly together. I see my father. He is sitting, leaning against the mud brick of our hut, in a beam of sunlight. When I ask him what he is doing, he tells me he's 'soaking up the rays' and I ask him if this is like taking a bath and he laughs.

I hear a roar.

I open my eyes and see the creature, an arm's length away. It is not looking at me, though. It has turned its confused gaze back to the top of the stairs, where the roar came from. There is another creature and it is one I recognise: the feral with the black streak in his white hair.

He stands, backlit by the mid-morning sun, his mouth wide. He has Matthew's knife in his hand. I can't understand the rush of relief I have at his appearance, as if being devoured by two of these things will be better than one, but in a world full of new and horrible encounters, this feral is at least familiar.

The first creature turns back to me. His mouth stretches open – the closest it might get to a smile – and the stench of him wafts over me. I gag. Is this going to be the last thing I smell, this distorted face going to be the last human I will ever see?

I want to close my eyes, to go back to the memories. The creature's orange eyes are on me now and I can't look away. I will fight it. I will fight my death.

Another roar.

The creature with the black streak leaps down the stairs and throws himself at the other. The first catches my shoulder with his taloned hand at the same moment. I am knocked off balance and tumble into the water. The bundle of fighting creatures falls in on top of me.

The weight of Bayat's cloak drags me down. I open my eyes and see only patches of blackness. Something is holding my ankle, I feel the sting of talons digging into my flesh. I am being pulled down by the creature. We are going to the bottom.

I am nothing and I am everything.

I am the darkness in the seas.

I am the water.

I am the wetness.

I am me.

My ears roar. Bubbles erupt around me. I sink further, down, down to the soft, soft, earth. I open my eyes. The cave again. Bayat. My hunter, smiling. He reaches out and touches my cheek. I feel the heat of his finger-tips on my skin. I see myself in his eyes, my ocean-touched face. I do not shiver. I am strong this time and watch as he is transformed into the great cat. The cougar's eyes bore into me, her soul speaking to me. She leans over and whispers: 'Chimera'.

The cave is gone and I am the sky, looking down at all below me: the shimmering city and the blue harbour. Screams and a terrible whistling sound.

On the other side of the water there is a great fire ball, tumbling along, following the path we have travelled and I yell out to Fatima to 'run, run,

run!' But my mouth is not working, I am the sky and I can only watch.

And the figures below are not us. They are men, women, children, thousands of them, being consumed by the red flames, turned to piles of ashes in an instant.

On the other side, over the bridge, creeping creatures are emerging from the tunnels below the city and they are grabbing the bewildered people, sinking teeth into them. Men with machine guns spray the crowds with bullets, not caring who they hit. Growling and roaring mix with human cries of agony.

I am moving up, away from the screams and the terrible whistling sound and in the distance, I can see the mouth of my river, my home ...

I open my eyes and kick. I kick ferociously at the something that is gripping my ankle. The cloak is off me, lost in the black water. I kick again and again and feel the weight lift off. I can see a glimmer of light above me. My breath is almost out, my energy fading. I use the last of my strength to push, push, push into the air, gulping in the wonder of still being alive.

A shadow looms. A splash next to me. I think of the ferals but can't manage to swim away. Arms wrap around me and a familiar voice says, 'We've got you, Pandora. We've got you'.

I feel myself lifted out of the water and my body is placed on the ground. Except the ground is moving … The strangest sensation, this intense rocking. In half-consciousness, I look up at white, the sail billowing above me.

'One of them is still alive!' Oyan calls.

I sit up. A gust of coldness hits me in the face and I bang my shoulder on the side of the boat, thrown off balance more than I expected. Pain rushes through me.

Emmaline is lying on the floor of the boat next to me. She is wet through and shivering.

'Emmaline?'

She opens her eyes for a moment and I gasp when I see her eyes have gone back to black.

'Fight it, Emmaline, fight it,' I whisper into her ear, hoping somehow she will hear me. She closes her eyes again.

'Shoot it!' I hear Matthew yell and I try to stand, but fall backwards onto the bench seat. Titus is at the back of the boat, trying to steer. Matthew is at the front, trying to re-attach the small sail to the pole. Both Oyan and Bayat are on the left side, their bows and arrows raised and drawn.

The group of ferals from the art gallery stand on the stone steps, glaring out at us. The body of the creature that had come for me is floating towards them, its back with Matthew's knife sticking out of it. The feral with the black streak is paddling back towards land, though not towards the group. I realise this is the creature they are planning to kill.

Bayat raises his bow.

'Don't, Bayat!' I scream and he swings around, the arrow now pointed at me.

'Why not?' he demands.

'He ... saved me!'

'He?' Oyan sneers. 'They aren't human, river girl.'

He raises his bow and shoots an arrow towards the creature. It plunges into the water, wide of its target. Oyan swears.

Bayat swings back to the water, aiming again at the creature.

'Please!' I yell, hardly knowing why.

Bayat continues to aim his arrow.

'Lost your nerve?' Oyan jeers.

Bayat shoots, the arrow spinning out into the water, just clipping the edge of the creature's shoulder. He looks back at us, then dives down.

I watch as the creature with the black streak reaches the shore, a mountain arrow in his hand, and scrambles up and over the stone wall, slinking back into the city.

Matthew has managed to tie down the small sail and Titus has mastered the steering as we pass through the heads of the harbour. We are suddenly out in the open and the air is tangy and wild. I watch the coastline passing by, amazed at our speed.

Why had the River People never built boats to use on the water? It seems ridiculous we haven't done such a thing. I would have to ask my father why when we got home. I remember him telling me how much I loved being rocked as a baby, how he and my mother had to do shifts to make sure I was swaying, to keep me asleep. I hadn't really understood what he was talking about. As I feel the boat moving beneath me, I get it. This motion is totally natural to me.

I let myself stay in this peaceful state a moment. Try not to think of Fatima. Try not to worry about Emmaline.

I look over to Matthew clinging to the side of the boat. His face is still green.

Bayat comes to sit next to me, close enough so our fingers are touching lightly together. I lean forward to watch the water passing below, the deep blue beneath is like a promise: deadly and full of possibility.

He slowly moves his fingers so they are resting on top of mine. I feel the warmth of his skin once again.

'When you were under the water,' Bayat speaks quietly so the others can't hear. 'Matthew and Titus blamed it on me. They said we should have fought the creatures instead of running away.'

'I had another vision,' I whisper back. 'Whilst I was under.'

I definitely don't want Matthew to hear.

'What was it?'

'I don't remember it all.' This is a lie. I can't bring myself to describe the creatures coming out of the tunnels, my realisation that they have been in the city since The Burning. 'There was the word: Chimera. Does that mean anything to you?'

'Chimera?' He blinks and I'm certain he recognises the word. He pauses for too long. 'No, nothing.'

I'm sure he is lying. Since I've just done the same, I don't push it. Not now.

We both turn back to looking at the deepening

colours of the cliff-faces. I let Bayat's hand slip off mine.

In the afternoon, Emmaline wakes up. I have been watching over her and feel intense relief when the eyes that open are her normal blue. Her fingernails have also returned to normal.

'What's happened?' Her voice is dry.

I help her to sit up and sip at a flask of water. It is the last left, but I know she needs it the most of all of us. She winces as she moves her left arm.

'We ran into some ... problems.'

Oyan snorts. 'That's one way of putting it.'

Matthew tells Emmaline what has happened and she looks down at her hands, examining them like they aren't her own.

'But I am cured?' she asks.

'Yes, definitely,' Matthew responds emphatically.

I don't mention the return of the strange eyes as we were leaving the harbour, nor the fact that I'm sure I can still see an orange trace in her skin. I don't want to scare her, or any of us, but I'm not completely convinced she is safe.

Darkness falls and we agree to anchor. We are not good enough sailors to guide the boat at night, without the shore to help us navigate.

We all find a spot to try to curl into but there is not enough room to lie down. I listen to the breathing of each of us in turn and know we are all awake. I would like to start a conversation, to try to return us to the night when we teased Caro about the naming of the Mountain People. But as soon as I think of it, I worry for Caro's mother, and Caro himself. Has he been taken by the sickness too?

I can't think of being as light-hearted as we were that night, not when we have left Fatima behind, not when we are so close to returning, to seeing the truth. All this time, I know we've been blocking out what might be waiting at the village and the tribe. For as long as we had been going away from it, we could let it be anything we wanted it to be. Remember it in a rosy haze, as it was before the disease. The closer we get, the harder it is to keep up the illusion. And what will I tell Fatima's parents, Whisper and Bren? And Cassie?

I close my eyes and listen again to the breathing:

maybe a few have fallen asleep. Maybe Bayat? Maybe Oyan? I can't tell the difference.

In my head, I see the feral with the black streak in his hair throwing himself at the other creature. Why did he do that? Was he really saving me? Why hadn't I wanted them to shoot him? Gratitude, I guess.

But if the creature can think – act like a hero – then what else might he be able to do? Are the creatures really safely contained in the city? They've been there since The Burning, but will they stay there forever?

'We cannot think of forever,' Theodore had once said. 'We can only think of the next generation.'

But if so much can change in such a short time, who is to say it can't all change?

22

Matthew, Emmaline, Titus and I recognise the entrance to our river as soon as it comes into view. We haven't come down to the sea all that often – this is outside our boundaries – but we still know the land well enough to spot the familiar shore-line.

All four of us call out to Bayat at the rudder.

'Go in! Go in!'

'That's our river!'

'Turn, turn!'

'We're almost home!'

Somehow he gets the overlapping messages and the boat veers in. We sail into the wide gaping mouth of the river. Here, the waters are still deep enough to not risk running into rocks or sandbars. But we know this cannot last long and have already jointly decided to be cautious, to secure it further out and swim to shore.

'Throw the anchor out!' Bayat yells. I feel my shoulders drop and realise how tense I have been all day, constantly worried we wouldn't make it, the sails would rip and we would be stranded.

Emmaline, Matthew, Titus and Oyan jump into the deep water, swimming with the bags on their heads and carrying the bows and arrows to the shore. Bayat and I wait until last. I'm the strongest swimmer and we have agreed he'll hand me the ZarVex to carry across.

'Good luck!' Matthew calls. Back on solid ground, he looks much healthier, the greenish glow diminishing with every passing moment.

'Be careful, river girl!' Oyan unhelpfully shouts.

I dive in and feel the coldness against my legs. It is just like the day of the Blossoming, although the water is too deep for me to see the bottom, and the river stones. Still, it is my river.

When I come back up, paddling on the surface, Bayat is leaning over the boat with the precious bag.

He hands it to me. Its weight surprises me and, for a moment, I think it's going to tip out of my hands and plunge into the water. I readjust my grip and hold it on the top of my head, kicking out to where the others are waiting.

Behind me, I hear the splash as Bayat jumps in to follow me.

By the time we are ready to start the last leg of our journey, with sodden clothes and having eaten a pretty pathetic snack of scavenged berries, it is already evening. None of us can imagine sleeping and we start walking, even if darkness might force us to stop shortly after.

I know it is at least a half day further to our village and it is maddening to not be able to get there quickly. Soon enough, the sun drops away and we know it will be stupid to risk stumbling along in the pitch blackness of the forest.

No one suggests making a fire, there are no clearings in this dense peninsula anyway, and we are far enough away from the mountains to not run the risk of encountering cougars. We lie down on the thickly leafed floor and wait.

In the grey light of pre-dawn, I sit up, momentarily confused as to where I am and what I am supposed to be doing. Somehow, I must have fallen asleep and I feel a rush of guilt: how many hours have we lost because of my lapse? Only as I stretch my cramped neck do I realise the others are sleeping too and I am, in fact, the only one awake. Curled or sprawled next to the trees they sat against last night, they have all succumbed to the bone weariness our travels have brought to us, even though we had vowed last night we'd never be able to sleep so close to our destination. How inconsistent we are, how much we kid ourselves we know our bodies and minds, how easily we can change, from one instant to the next.

Enough. No time.

'Come on everyone!' I clap my hands loudly. 'It's light! Let's get moving!'

There is something deeply satisfying about yelling into Oyan's ear, causing the startled jerking of his head.

'Okay, Pan, we get the idea,' Matthew grumbles and I stop my teacher-like clapping.

There's no question of eating. We start to make our way through the woods.

Despite the sun coming up, it is still tough going. The ground is covered in shadows and, although we start out fast, as if we can run all the way home, pretty soon we slow down, having to watch for tree roots, unstable patches of pine spindles and jutting rocks. There is no path, this isn't an area anyone travels through regularly, and we just have to keep stumbling on, hoping we will soon come to more familiar territory.

'Can't be long now,' Titus says, just as we emerge into a clearing I recognise. There, to the left, is the inlet of the river Fat and I had once named 'Ophelia's hole', after pretending to drown ourselves there when we were ten notches on the Growing Tree, romantically inspired by a telling of the *Hamlet* story in one of our lessons. The memory churns me up again.

To the right is the pathway which leads to the secret tuber field: a patch of land kept distant from the village and only tended by the most trusted. When I was younger I'd thought this was because the tubers were so important to our diet, only later did I realise it is because the tubers give us root-juice.

'We're almost there,' I whisper, worried that speaking too loudly will break the dream, I'll wake up and find we are still on the boat, days away, we will back at the moment when we abandoned Fatima.

Emmaline takes the lead, following the now clear pathway. Oyan, Bayat, Titus and Matthew follow and

I find myself at the back of the line. I don't have the energy to worry about this or, maybe, I have grown up enough not to let it get to me, and I stick to the quickened pace we are now moving at. I notice how the path is not as clear as it should be. We have to climb over fallen branches and move aside low hanging bushes. There hasn't been the usual upkeep of our pathways through the forest.

Finally, we see smoke rising above the canopy. Before I can even take in the sweet smell of burning wood, we are walking up Tareen Lane, towards the Great Hall.

We know immediately things are bad. The village is frighteningly quiet, no sounds of breakfast preparation, no whistling or singing. At least, the goateeps are still bleating.

Across the opening of the hall hangs a large piece of goateep skin. A curtain. Why? We have never chosen concealment before. What needs to be hidden now?

We huddle together in a group, unsure what to do next. I had not expected a hero's welcome, but I had expected some kind of acknowledgement, had assumed someone would be on the lookout for us. Have they given up on us? Are they all gone? Dead?

We hear movement behind the curtain. Omar pushes back the skin and gapes out at us. His eyes are tired and bloodshot, his lips cracked from dryness, his chin over-run by a beard. I am reminded of the old man back in the city.

'Matthew?' he croaks.

'Yes,' his son says simply.

As they embrace, I push aside the curtain and stumble into the Great Hall. A fire burns brightly in the pit, smoke billowing from the giant logs I can see have been thrown there. This is not the usual way we burn, using small faggots to minimise the smoke, and I have to blink rapidly to keep the sting out of my eyes.

When they finally adjust, I understand why the rest of the village is so quiet.

Everyone is here. Even the young ones.

23

I weave my way through the sick bodies, towards the space where I last saw my father. Behind me, I'm vaguely aware of the others coming in, of their sick realisation, like mine, that all of the village has been taken by the disease. Though I know I should already be administering the drug as quickly as possible, I am too selfish to simply begin. I need to comfort my father. I need to see my mother's reassured face, a smile of pride on it.

But it is not my father lying on the spot where he fell on the day of the Blossoming. Instead, mother of three, Verity, lies in a pool of sweat, breathing shallowly, her long brown hair fanned out around her head. Curled around her are the small, sleeping bodies of her children Taquin, Neena and Tyrone. With relief, I realise there is no evidence of the disease on their faces and understand the presence of so many young ones in the hall has more to do with necessity than complete plague. It looks like the adults left were too exhausted to look after the children separately.

I still cannot see my father or mother. This can't be happening. I refuse to accept their absence for what it might mean.

'They're not here.'

Bayat is by my side. He doesn't give me the reassurance I want. 'You need to start injecting.'

'Where's my mother and father?' I whisper into the horrible silence. The only reply is the grunts and groans of the sick.

'Pandora, we need to focus on those who are here. We need to save them.'

Even in my pain, he reaches me. Better not to think about the future, concentrate on the now.

With a feeling of numbness, I draw ZarVex into the needle and use Verity as my second injecting specimen. Her children stir awake as I am preparing myself and I have to explain how I'm not going to hurt their mother. Neena, the eldest, with seven notches, nods solemnly and holds her brothers' hands, a triumvirate of care encircling their mum's head. I push the needle's tip into the fat of Verity's shoulder, there is no time to find a vein. I want to cry when her face visibly breaks from its fevered state, her eyes opening for just a moment before closing again, turning her body to the side as if settling into a comfortable sleep for the first time in a long while. Taquin giggles.

Titus asks me quietly if I will please do his parents next and I can't believe how restrained he's been. Atticus and Corrine lie side by side but once they are done, Titus doesn't stay with them. He continues to help me, moving the ill into position and holding their arms down. Bayat and Oyan watch carefully, storing up knowledge.

I move from patient to patient, giving the sick a vial each, though I discover some of them are broken despite all our efforts. I use up fifteen. Fifteen? Where is everyone else? I watch as Whisper's face softens with the ZarVex, thinking of Fatima. Her father, Bren, is not here, nor do I see her sister Cassie.

Through all this, Omar and Matthew don't return and we only rediscover Emmaline when we find her sitting next to Theodore.

'I'll do it,' she says, her hands visibly shaking as she tries to take the needle from me.

'I don't think that's a good idea,' I say.

'I'll do it,' she repeats, gritting her teeth together.

I hand it to her and watch as she jabs it into

his father's shoulder, the shake gone. We watch as Theodore does what all the others have done: lets out an audible sigh of relief, jerking into consciousness for only a moment before rolling over towards slumber.

Emmaline lowers her head and I understand why she is weeping. This is the scene I had pictured for myself.

I stand up. Omar and Matthew are walking towards us. In the smoke, my eyes are watering and I see the grimness on Matthew's face through a veil of tears. He is coming to tell me the news. He is coming to tell me my parents are dead. I am too tired. Too hungry. Too weak. Blood drains away from my head. I am dizzy. I fall into blackness.

I wake. Around me, the warmth of an unfamiliar cloak, its hair rubbing against my bare skin. I turn onto my back and open my eyes to see an all-too-familiar sight: the roof of our hut. If I glance over to the wall, I will see the empty space where my parents used to sleep. I do not do it, following the hairline crack running from halfway up the wall to the chimney. Is it my imagination or has it grown longer since I left? Has everything truly torn apart?

Only slowly do I register a sound, pulling the cloak away from my ears, removing myself from the cocoon I've woken into.

'There are only thirty-five vials left. Less than the tribe might need apparently ...'

I jerk my head so quickly I send a wave of pain through my neck muscle and cry out. Immediately, two figures rush over.

'Pan, are you okay?'

'Where does it hurt?'

My mother and father kneel down next to me. I stare at them.

'Pan?'

'My love?'

I am holding my breath. I can't think of what to say to them. To put into words all I have felt, all I am feeling.

I breathe out.

'Why weren't you waiting for me?'

It's the stupidest thing to say. A childish accusation.

'We have been, Pan. It's just we had to ...' My father stops. He looks at my mother.

I swallow. I don't know if I can take the news yet.

'Did they give you ZarVex?' I ask Hector, sad I have missed his miraculous rehabilitation.

'No, they didn't need to.'

'Your father recovered a week ago. I thought he was one of the worst cases for a while there but it turned out his journey was going along the path to recovery, not ...'

'Death.'

'Hector ...' She puts her hand on his forearm in one of those gestures I've always loved, this easy grace between them.

'We can't hide it from her, Zaana.'

I almost start laughing at the idea of them trying to protect me. Don't they know what I've been through? What I've seen?

No, of course they don't.

To them, I am the same girl who disappeared down the Dead End all those days ago.

'We lost another seventeen while you were gone.'

'Seventeen?'

'Twenty dead in total.'

Twenty? *Twenty*? A third of the village ...

'But you've saved all the rest,' my father quickly tries to reassure me.

'We should've travelled faster.'

I remember talking about how the hours were

passing and who might die while we sat waiting. I'd been right.

'Cassie?' I hadn't seen her in the hall. But she had been well when we left …

'She's alive. But Bren … died yesterday. That's where we were. Digging his grave.'

Oh Fatima. She would never have a chance to tell her father about the bridge. My eyes fill with tears, even as I fight them. I want to show my parents how much I've grown up but I'm dissolving like a young one.

'You did an incredible job.' My mother wraps her arms around me.

I hold onto her, clinging desperately to the idea we haven't failed them completely.

'Are you proud of me?' I whisper through the tears.

She nods her head. Only gradually do I realise she is shaking and, for the first time in my memory, my mother is crying.

My father puts his arms around us both. We are a circle again, unbroken.

'Pan?' Matthew has appeared at our hut's entrance. 'Bayat and Oyan need to go.'

My parents and I stand and follow Matthew out into the open. The four of us walk quickly to the Great Hall where Bayat and Oyan wait. Everyone looks so tired and I know the Mountain People still have much further to travel.

Emmaline and Titus emerge from the Great Hall, carrying the bag of the remaining ZarVex between them. It looks almost ceremonial, this slow solemn march holding a prized object.

Oyan takes the bag and carefully slings it over his shoulders. I would have preferred Bayat to take it, but this isn't the time to start an argument.

'Time to go,' Oyan says and strides off, towards the Dead End. He stops, waiting, at the top of the path.

Bayat looks at him but doesn't move. The five of us stand awkwardly together, my parents hanging back, as if they know this is a special farewell.

I offer my hand to Emmaline and she takes it and offers hers to Matthew who extends his to Titus who takes Bayat's. Bayat takes my other hand. The five of us become another circle. I feel Fatima's absence and I'm sure all of us are thinking of her.

'Good luck,' Titus says in that strange, serious voice he adopts in times of stress.

'Thank you,' Bayat says. I squeeze his hand and

I feel Emmaline squeezing mine and I know we are trying to send each other strength. Enough to get through the tough times ahead. A third of our village gone. What will Bayat find in the mountains?

We drop hands.

Bayat turns to me and I stare hard at him, swallowing, making sure I don't cry this time. I hate the idea of not seeing him every morning, as we have for what seems like forever. Not to mention the possibility we might not see each other again. I can't think about it. I break my gaze and look over his shoulder, at Oyan and the path they are about to walk down.

'I have to get back to my tribe and save as many as I can.'

I know he needs to go.

I stand by as Emmaline hugs him, as do Titus and Matthew.

Bayat puts his arms around me, pulling my body close to his and then letting go, quickly and without intensity. It's a fleeting hug, like something you'd give a person you hardly know. I want to grab him again, make him hold me, but I'm still too proud.

He turns and picks up his own bag, slinging it over his shoulder. I stand, just a little bewildered. This is all I'm going to get?

Bayat straightens, adjusting the bag and, with an intense look at me, takes my hand with both of his. He glances over my shoulder and I know Matthew is hovering there. As Bayat draws his fingers along my own, I feel the weight of what he has given me and close my palm around it.

'I'll see you,' he says.

He turns and walks towards Oyan who waves. I stay fixed to the spot, watching as they disappear into the tunnel of the forest, imprinting every muscle's movement into my mind. When Bayat is gone from sight, Matthew places his hand on the small of my back.

I look down, opening my fingers a little to reveal what Bayat has given me: half of the river stone. It sits on my palm, the shorn edge gleaming in the sunlight. I think of the time it would have taken to cleave it in two and wonder when he managed to do it.

I close my fingers around the half-stone, feeling its warmth on my skin.

I'd like to go and sleep but the exhaustion I've seen in Omar's face and the deep black bags under my parents' eyes show there isn't time to indulge myself.

'What needs to be done?' I ask my parents.

'All the sick are sleeping and, from what Emmaline has told us about the effects of ZarVex, it is likely they will sleep for the rest of the day.' My mother speaks crisply, as if addressing the village, the remnants of her tears seemingly disappeared. 'If you four could gather up the young ones and give them breakfast. Hopefully, by tomorrow we can have some of them back in their own huts.'

She doesn't talk about the orphans and I don't talk about Fatima, grateful that poor Whisper is under the effect of ZarVex and can't ask questions yet.

We sit crossed-legged with the young ones under the shade of the Growing Tree. It is a huge oak which grows at the far-east side of the village. Each child born since The Burning has a line of notches gouged into its side, the birthday ritual is to come here and watch your parents cut a new mark into the knobbly bark. I can see my notches, even and deep, gouged out by my father, running up above my name: PAN. Next to mine are Fatima's.

The children, ranging from two to eleven notches, are eerily quiet, so different from how they were before the disease came. I watch them, seeing the traces of their grief. Freya and Fee have lost both their mother and father, as have Fern and Dell. Mohan and Tena still have their mother, a fact shared with Verity's children while Marcus and Millie have their father still. They all sit closely together, the siblings giving each other comfort.

It is only Hope, the single child of Eva and Stratum, who both died, who sits alone.

'Drink your milk,' Emmaline encourages and cups rise dutifully to lips. I have to stop myself from checking on Emmaline every other moment. I'm worried about the presence of the feral virus inside her. She still has the strips of skin wrapped around her wound so I can't see if the punctures have closed up or not.

Hope brings me her emptied cup, handing it to me with a pitifully thin arm.

'What's going to happen to me, Pan?' she asks in her five-year-old voice. She has a faint lisp, the 's' running long as her tongue gets caught in-between her teeth.

I open my arms and she comes to sit on my lap, without any real enthusiasm. It is just another thing she is expected to do. I've never paid much attention to these young ones and they don't yet have any kind of relationship with me.

'We are going to protect you,' I whisper into her ear. I have a memory of Matthew saying almost the same thing to me, in the forest, right after Bayat kissed me. I glance over to him and he catches my eye. He smiles sadly.

'You?' Hope asks, sceptically looking up at me.

'All of us. The village. We are going to take care of one another.'

She nods, seeming to accept her fate.

After looking after the young ones, I spend the day reclaiming one of the neglected fields, weeding it and preparing it for sowing. We don't know when the rains will come and there might not be enough time to cultivate seedlings resistant to the deluge. But we have to try and I relish the opportunity to work side-by-side with my father, the two of us sweating together, the physical work helping to drive away all the dark thoughts.

That night, my first back in our hut, I close my eyes expecting sleep to come easily, I am so tired, but it doesn't. I feel the emptiness of the village like a weight. I turn from side to side, trying to find a place to be comfortable, an escape. But there is no escape. I know I have to take the boat and go in search of Fatima as soon as I can. I have to tell her about her father. And I keep seeing the creatures, emerging from the tunnels below the city and spreading out across the land. And the face of the first one I killed and the old man's face as we left him and the creature with the black streak slowly backing away from me.

I open my eyes again.

My parents are both sleeping, wrapped in one another's arms.

In my hand, I hold my half of the river stone. I rub the edge of it with my thumb, wanting to find some comfort. One day I hope it will re-join with its other half.

Until then, I try to dream.

Author's Note

The Nature Needs Half movement, established in 2009, believes we can stop the sixth mass extinction event we are currently heading towards if we protect approximately 50% of each of the 846 eco-regions that provide habitat for all of Earth's biodiversity. For more information go to www.natureneedshalf.org

About the Author

Photo: Silvergum Photography

Rachel Hennessy is the award-winning author of two novels of contemporary fiction: *The Quakers* (Wakefield Press, 2008) and *The Heaven I Swallowed* (Wakefield Press, 2013). Her first novel, about a group of obsessive teenagers, was described by John Birmingham as 'un-put-down-able' and was winner of the Adelaide Festival's Best Unpublished Manuscript Award. Her second novel was Runner Up in the *Australian/Vogel Award*, long-listed for the Nita B Kibble Award and described by *Australian Aboriginal Studies* as 'an important book'. Rachel lives in Melbourne with her partner and their two young daughters.

MidnightSun Publishing

We are a small, independent publisher based in Adelaide, South Australia. Since publishing our first novel, Anna Solding's *The Hum of Concrete* in 2012, MidnightSun has gone from strength to strength.

We create books that are beautifully produced, unusual, sexy, funny and poignant. Books that challenge, excite, enrage and overwhelm. When readers tell us they have lost themselves in our stories, we rejoice in a job well done.

MidnightSun Publishing aims to reach new readers every year by consistently publishing excellent books. Welcome to the family!

midnightsunpublishing.com